2   W9-AEY-960

A12902 033918

BLACK MEDIA ENTERPRISE PRESENTS

KING 2 Blood on the Crown

A novel by Tremayne Johnson

I.C.C. LIBRARY

PS.
3601
.056
K564
2012
c. 2

Written by: Tremayne Johnson

Cover design by: Greg Itis for DZYNiD INC.

Category: Fiction/Urban Life

Copyright© 2012 by T. Johnson

2/15 Amazon 8.99

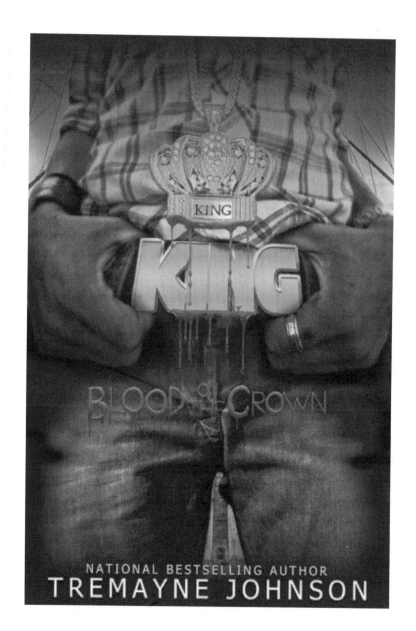

KING

BLOOD & CROWN

NATIONAL BESTSELLING AUTHOR
TREMAYNE JOHNSON

This novel is a work of fiction. Any resemblances to real people, living or dead, actual events, establishments, organizations, and/or locales are intended to give the fiction a sense of reality and authenticity. Other names, characters, places and incidents are either products of the author's imagination or are used fictitiously, as are those fictionalized events and incidents that involve real persons and did not occur or are set in the future.

This book is dedicated to

Raymond 'Razor' Harris

We love you my G! S.I.P

Tremayne Johnson contrives a vividly, detailed canvas out of words that literally spring off the pages at you. Descriptive scenes, clever plot formation and intoxicating story lines are sure to keep the reader enthralled. Some of his favorites are Donald Goines, Chester Himes, James Patterson and David Weaver. To date he is the author of four Bestselling novels.

Contacts:

www.tremaynej.com

Facebook.com/tremaynej

Twitter.com/GS914

Also available:

A Drug Dealer's Dream

KING

The Union 1

The Union 2

CHAPTER ONE

Dear Butch,

I heard you the man out there in the town now. You know Deon (KING) was like a little brother to me right? I never liked you Butch and I still don't. I should'a put that knife through your heart instead of your back, but fuck it... I'm sure I'll get another chance.

I'm 'bout to touch the streets in a minute. If I was you, I'd run now because when I catch you I'ma stick my knife so far in ya gut, you gon' be shittin' stainless steel for a month. Word to Mommy!

I'm comin' for that crown Butch... it rightfully belongs to me!

Yours truly,
That Nigga, Jay-Roc!

Butch sneered as he sat in his wheelchair looking down at the yellow piece of paper signed by the same person that was responsible for putting him in the very seat he would be sitting in for the remainder of his life. Each and every time the name came across his mind, a darting pain would shoot through his back, his lip would quiver and he would cringe.

He spat on the piece of paper, balled it in his fist and grilled the young gunner who brought it to his attention. "Who gave you this?"

"This lil' redbone bone bitch from over on Halsey."

"Halsey?" Butch shook his head and unraveled the paper. "Yo, what's this word right here?"

The young gunner bent down to see what word Butch was having trouble with.

"This one right here," Butch raised his right hand and planted a fierce slap to the side of the young boys face. "Now go find the bitch that gave you this shit or the next time I see you we got a problem."

The young gunner grabbed his cheek and bent down to pick up the letter. "But Butch... I—"

Seeing the chrome handle of Butch's .45 silenced anything else he thought about saying. He swallowed the lump of pride stuck in his throat and turned on his heels to exit. "I told you we should'a let that bitch do it." He shoved his partner and they walked out the front door.

Butch was enraged. "Lock the fuckin' door, Red!" he wheeled himself through the kitchen and into the living room of the two bedroom project apartment. "You read that shit?"

Red had a smirk on his face. "Hell yeah I read that shit."

"So what the fuck you smilin' for nigga?"

Red played with the toothpick in his mouth. "I thought it was bullshit when I heard it, but I guess it's true... Roc comin' home, what's your plan?"

"Plan?" Butch lifted the weapon from his lap and cocked it. "Find out when that nigga get released." He gritted his teeth and held his composure. "I wanna be at the gate the day they let that nigga out. I got somethin' sweet for his ass."

Red snatched the paper off the coffee table, glanced at it and then tossed it in Butch's lap. "I think it's a lil' too late for that."

Butch eyed the article:

RAP SUPERSTAR WELCOMES HOME LONGTIME FRIEND AFTER WINNING HIS APPEAL

It was a picture of Jay-Roc standing with a multi-selling platinum recording artist from Brooklyn.

"This is today's paper?" he asked.

"Yesterday."

"So why am I jus' now seein' this?"

"I don't know Butch, the shit been sittin' on the table all day. I jus' saw it myself."

A knock at the door made both men turn their heads.

"Who is it?" Red made his voice deeper than usual.

"Jay-Roc!"

Butch and Red looked at each other and then Red went to open the door.

"Hol' up nigga..." Butch slightly pulled the barrel back to make sure a bullet was in the chamber. His hands were shaking and he was visibly nervous. "Fuck is wrong wit' this nigga... think he gon' come up in my joint..." he was rambling in a low tone. "Open the door Red."

Red looked through the peephole but couldn't see anything. "It's too dark to see who it is."

"Nigga jus' open the fuckin' door!"

When the door came open young Vic was standing in the hallway with a huge smile on his face and a newspaper in his hand. He stepped inside.

"Yo, Butch did you see your boy Jay-Roc in the-"

Butch moved so fast in his chair that Vic didn't know how to react. Before he knew it his back was pinned against the door and a pistol was pointed at his dick.

"You niggas think this Jay-Roc shit is a joke huh?" Butch was beyond heated. He felt disrespected, and when he felt disrespected his only reaction was to become disrespectful.

"Yo, Butch chill... I was jus' playin'." Vic whined.

"Shut up nigga." He shoved the barrel of the handgun into his nuts. "Strip!"

"Huh?" Vic's heart skipped a beat.

"Yeah, all of it, off... right now."

Red knew what was about to take place. He had seen it done on more than one occasion.

Vic unbuttoned his coat and stripped down to his boxer shorts.

"C'mon Butch, man..." Tears were building in the wells of his eyes.

"I said all of it nigga."

A droplet fell down Vic's cheek as he came out of his boxer shorts. He looked over to Red for some type of help, but Red turned his back and walked in the other direction.

Butch got pleasure out of humiliating people. He thrived off belittling the next person and making them feel unwanted. His own insecurities were to blame, but that's something he would never reveal to the world.

"I don't know what the fuck you lookin' at him for, that nigga can't help you. Red! Open the door."

Red didn't want to do it. His heart wasn't as cold as Butch's was and he tried his best to treat people with respect because that's the way his mother had raised him; which, by far was the total opposite of his counterpart.

"Butch, listen man," he tried to reason. "It's three-o-clock in the afternoon on Thanksgiving

Day. Don't you think this shit could be handled in a different manner?"

Butch cut his eyes at Red and tightened his lips. "Nigga, if I gotta tell you one more time to open that door, you gon' be takin' yo' shit off too."

Red wasn't about to inherit someone else's problem, so he did as he was told.

When they got downstairs, Vic was hesitant on stepping outside the lobby door in his birthday suit because he couldn't stomach the embarrassment. "Please, Butch don't make me go out there like this." he cried.

Red tried to make himself look good by grabbing the back of Vic's neck and pushing him out the door. "Walk nigga!" he got in close to his ear and whispered. "You better run when you get out there."

"Oh shit! Look at this nigga!" someone screamed out when they saw Vic come stumbling down the four steps to enter the building.

Vic covered himself with his hands and stood in front of the building shaking like a dope fiend going through withdrawal.

A drafty breeze flowed through the projects rustling the fresh autumn leaves that had fallen from the trees and covered the ground. It was Thanksgiving Day and the hood was packed.

"Yo Vic! You smokin' dust nigga!?" Another yelled.

The tenants, young and old started to form a crowd in the front of the building.

Butch made his way down the ramp holding the gun firmly in his grasp. "I'ma tell y'all niggas this shit one time... I don't tolerate disrespect." he pointed the gun in Vic's direction. "Get on your knees nigga."

Red attempted to stop him. "Butch!"

"Shut the fuck up Red!" his attention went back to Vic. "This nigga thought he could disrespect me and get away with it..."

"Yo, Butch let the lil' nigga go!" A female shouted.

Butch ignored her plea. "I want somebody to give this message to Jay-Roc."

Red turned his head and the rupture of the gun caused him to almost jump out of his skin.

"Oh shit!" One of the onlookers sang out.

The crowd scattered and Vic's naked body collapsed and hit the pavement hard. Blood from the hole in his head spilled into the cracks of the concrete while Butch just sat there, poised, with a malicious simper glued to his face. He knew the people wouldn't tell on him because of their fear of becoming the next victim, so he played on his power and continued to rule his streets with an iron fist.

———————

Five years ago Butch the Bully pulled the trigger of a double barreled shotgun and ended the young life of Brooklyn's King, Deon Toure. Since that day he's made a radical alteration to his lifestyle.

The drugs he once abused, mainly heroin; had become detrimental to his physical well-being and also his mental state of mind. The white, crystalline, narcotic powder was beginning to dismantle his livelihood and it took a harrowing experience for him to realize that he needed to make an adjustment.

After overdosing on a bag of pure, China white heron and almost flat lining; Butch decided to check himself into a drug rehabilitation clinic. It had come to the point where the drugs had taken total control over his life. He craved nothing other than the satisfaction of a needle in his arm and the sweet euphoria of dope running through his veins. His habit made him inferior to those who he knew feared him at one point; they now looked down on him and made a parody of what he used to be. His rankings declined in the streets and he was viewed as nothing but a fiend, a has-been; that nigga that 'had' it, but no longer has it; a certified bum-ass-nigga and this angered Butch. He wasn't accustomed to being treated in such a fashion because it was always him doing the bullying and ridiculing, but the tables had shifted and receiving a dose of his own medicine hit home hard. It made him take a good look at that person staring back at him in the mirror every morning. The strong, informing words of his mother reciting prayers from the pages of the bible were finally starting to settle in and for the first time Butch felt guilty about the things he had to resort to in order to maintain his high.

He finally understood that he reached his bottom the day he killed Deon because prior to the incident, Butch had gone to his mother's house and stole money from her purse. It was the first time he had ever done anything like it and while doing it he knew how wrong it was, but his addiction was in control.

Later that night, after the shooting; Butch went over to Flatbush Avenue and purchased a bundle of dope from one of the local hustlers. What he didn't know was Rahmeek had every dealer in the area waiting on his call. He knew Butch would be looking for a bag after committing the murder, so he put the word out and when the call came in the boys from Flatbush Avenue had a special surprise for the Bully.

Rahmeek had them put a bag of pure dope into the bundle that Butch would be buying in hopes that he would mainline the potent chemical and die from an overdose, but Butch was still breathing after half the bag and the only explanation they could come up with was that God had been holding his hand and it just wasn't his time to move on.

As he lay near death on that cold hospital bed, the only people by his side was his mother and Red. She had come to his aid each and every time, so his only choice was to be thankful and remorseful. The whirlwind of guilt inside of him was so tormenting that he could barely look into her eyes as a faint whisper seeped through his lips. "I'm sorry ma." he turned his head away.

Butch's mother was a small, aging woman whose beady eyes had crow's feet because she'd seen it all. She stared down at Butch with her browns and fixed her thin wrinkled lips to speak. "You got ta' change Butch... you got ta' make a change or else you gon' get yo' self killed out there in them streets." she placed her fragile hand on his. "You know the Lord don't condone those sinful ways you go about livin' and like I told you befo', it's gon' soon catch up to ya' and when it do... you gon' wish it didn't." her voice was delicate yet stern.

Butch's eyes were closed but the truth his mother spoke was vivid. There was no way he could continue staggering down the same path; it was too much. His heart wouldn't be able to handle it. He thought about all the wrong he had done and like flashes of light they appeared one by one in his mind's eye.

Every few seconds he would sit up and peek at the door anticipating the swarm of a battalion of blue suited police officers. But after countless hours they never showed up and for the moment Butch had literally gotten away with murder.

After two days in the hospital, the heroin withdrawal kicked in and it was the most excruciating pain that he would ever experience. Every time he closed his eyes he would relive the shocked expression on Deon's face before he squeezed the trigger. The resounding blast of the massive weapon continued to ring in his ears and the screams of the bystanders could be heard like he was still standing on the street. During the middle of the night Butch would jump out of his sleep in a panic stricken daze; sweating profusely, barely able to catch his breath. It was these same nights of terror that somewhat humbled him and caused him to examine his way of living. If God hadn't brought him home by now there had to be a reason.

The day the hospital released Butch he had a choice to make. It was either go back to the streets and continue thuggin' and druggin' or sign into an in-patient drug program and make the necessary adjustments to live a healthy lifestyle, but from the way things were looking, he was leaning more towards the direction he came from and his mother immediately sensed it.

"You think the Lord gon' let you keep doing this ta' yo' self Butch?" She stood at the foot of his bed while the nurse got him into his chair and gathered his belongings for him to leave. "He's giving you a second chance... you need ta' take advantage of it," when she noticed Butch wasn't paying attention, she cut her eyes to Red. "And you Michael," she said. "I know yo' folks done taught you better than that."

Red was seated in a chair beside the exit tapping his two hundred dollar suede loafers on the freshly waxed floor. His fitted slacks rose above his ankles showing the little man on the horse of his Polo dress socks, because despite having a heroin addiction, Red stayed sharp. He'd been that way since a child.

Out of respect he didn't say a word. He just listened.

"I don't know what y'all out there doin' but I sho' do know it ain't right and you know it too Michael, I can see it on ya' face."

As bad as he wanted it to be false, that statement couldn't have been any truer. The guilt was visible. He tried to disguise it, but it was too obvious.

"But Ms. Jones..."

"Don't *but* me Michael." she cut in. "This is it; this is the last time. I been comin' ta' y'alls rescue since y'all was lil' heathens runnin' 'round in these goddamn streets." She unbuttoned her trench coat and grabbed her smart phone from her purse. "I'm tired of it Butch. Y'all gon' send me ta' an early grave."

Butch finally looked up and saw her with the phone in her hand. "Who you callin' ma?"

"You know who I'm callin'." She reached in her purse again and fetched her reading glasses so she could see the directory in her phone.

"Ma, I ain't goin' to no rehab, I told you already..."

Throughout the year, leading up to the shooting, Ms. Jones had been pleading and begging her only son to get himself some help because the disease of addiction was scraping and eating away at his soul. The drugs were transforming him into one of *the devil's pawns* as she would say and it became unusually hard for her to witness his self-inflicted destruction and lack of respect for life. She hadn't raised him that way and she didn't have a clue as to where things went wrong; all she wanted to do was somehow correct it and make everything right.

"Oh yes you are." She replied, looking directly at him. "It's either gon' be this drug center or them streets... 'cause ya' ain't comin' back inta' my house with that nonsense."

Red giggled.

"And I don't know why you laughing Michael... 'cause you goin' too."

"Huh?"

"Huh my ass... ya' momma downstairs now, she got the van all gassed up for y'all."

Red jumped up and ran to the window to see if it was true, but the side of the building they were on faced the dumpsters.

Butch got comfortable in his chair and moved toward the exit. "I don't care ma... I ain't goin'."

"Goddamnit Butch!" She slammed the phone on the floor and tears instantly washed her face. "Yes you are!" she moved in close to him. "Don't you see this is killin' you Butch... all this pain and sufferin' you causin' it ain't jus' affectin' you; it's affectin' me too. It's killin' me..." her voiced got low and the tears fell faster.

Butch's heart got weak seeing the waterfall down his mother's cheeks. He had only seen her cry once before this and that was thirty years ago after a judge sentenced his father to life with no parole.

"Ma don't cry, please..." Butch dropped his head in shame.

"I can't do nothin' else but cry..."

At that moment Butch made a decision to listen and take heed to his mother's pleas. He thought about the few months away at the drug center being a blessing because he did need to escape the turmoil of the streets and regain a grip on his life. He could only imagine the type of regime he could construct under a sober state of mind. He rubbed shoulders and put in work with killers from every part of Brooklyn that was thirsty to be a part of something and the influence he had over easily manipulated people was powerful. The only thing he needed to do now was formulate a solid plan and a flawless execution.

He looked down at his hands; they were swollen and puffy like a pair of winter mittens, results from all the years of shooting dope into his veins. He glanced at his mother. "Aight ma... we gon' go..." and then he looked over at Red. "Checkmate..."

CHAPTER TWO

Jay-Roc paid the driver and jumped out the livery cab at the corner of 5th Avenue and 36th Street in Manhattan. He brushed a hand over his freshly cut waves and glanced up at the morning sun. Taking a moment, he inhaled a chest full of polluted city air and then smiled. He smiled illustrious for receiving the Lord's blessing of a second chance at life—for his freedom and for the opportunity to avenge his friend's death.

The bustle of the everyday pedestrians in the crowded city shocked him because he wasn't accustomed to the speed of the outside world. Everything was slower where he had just come from. He'd spent long days and sleepless nights confined to a 9 ½ by 12 foot cell where he was told when to move and when not to, but after being incarcerated for ten years, Jay-Roc was finally a free man and back on the same streets he once ruled.

It was his third day home and he was headed to a recording studio to meet up with one of his close friends, Troy Carter aka Babe Boy.

When he reached the building with the big number thirty six on it he entered and approached the information desk. "*Chung King* Studios please?" he said to the attendant. She made him put his signature on a sign-in sheet and then directed him to the elevator.

Jay-Roc stepped off the elevator on the third floor and pressed the buzzer that was on the wall.

A voice came over the speaker system. "Who is it?"

"Roc." He answered and was buzzed in.

Chung King Studios is the premier facility for some of the world's most exclusive entertainers to record their records and movie scores. The V.I.P list ranged from *Aaliyah* to *Aretha* and from *Jada Kiss* to *Jimmy Hendrix*. At any given time you could walk into Chung King and run into your favorite Hip Hop or R&B artist. It was the norm.

Another door buzzed after he entered the first and Jay-Roc walked into the lounge area of the large, well-furnished studio where gold and platinum plaques lined the walls from top to bottom displaying the array of talent that once stood in the same spot he was standing in.

He looked up when someone came out from the back room.

"Wassup Jay-Roc?" A young kid in a fitted cap with skinny jeans and a tight sweatshirt extended his arm for a handshake but Jay-Roc didn't respond. He just stared. "You don't remember me huh? I use to stay on Gates by the pizza shop."

The kid was beginning to look familiar to Jay-Roc. "Lil' Roland... Sneek's brother?"

"Yup, that's me." He extended his arm once more and Jay-Roc dapped him and gave him some hood love.

"Damn boy..." He stepped back and got a good look at the young man he hadn't seen since he was a child. "You got big as hell. What's good?"

Roland pulled a Dutch Master from his pocket and ripped the wrapper off. "You already know my G... we livin' that rap life." he dumped the guts into a small garbage can that was in the corner and fetched a zip lock bag of weed from his pants pocket. "You aint on parole right... you smokin'?"

"Nah, I'm good. I gotta keep a clear head."

Roland nodded in agreement. "True, true... I feel you on that. I need to quit smokin' this shit my damn self." He proceeded to roll up his weed. "Damn my G, how long you been gone?"

"Ten years..."

"Shit! Ten years?" he couldn't believe it. "That's too muhfuckin' long for a nigga not be gettin' no ass, but I'm glad you made it home safe my G. I know a bunch of niggas that went up state or to the feds and they ain't gon' never see the light of day again. It's fucked up but what they say is the truth... *'you fuck wit these streets and the only places you end up is in a casket or a cell.'*"

23

"Absolutely." Jay-roc took a seat on one of the couches. "There's consequences that follow every decision we make and if you a stand up nigga, you put that 'S' on your chest and play the game with the hand they deal you; ain't no way around it."

Roland quickly took a seat in the leather chair that was directly in front of Jay-Roc. It wasn't every day that he got to hear the words of a real O.G.; one who was actually in the streets, putting in work. "What was it like in there Roc?" he questioned.

Jay-Roc anticipated this particular question. It was human nature for people to want to know about prison—especially when they have no intentions on making any visits.

He smirked, scratched his head and then took a deep breath. "To sum it up... it's a livin' hell. Imagine being told what to do, when to do it... and how to do it. And then to top it off... all that by some alien ass cracker from west bumbblefuck somewhere screamin' in your face, standing over you while you piss and eyeing you while you strip down to nothing."

Roland had begun to light his blunt but he paused and pondered what Jay-Roc was saying. "That shit is crazy Roc... I don't know how you was able to handle that but you already know." he flicked the lighter and let the orange flame hit the tip of the blunt. "The streets talkin'."

"And... what they sayin?" Jay-Roc asked, even though he already knew what the answer was.

"C'mon Roc..." Roland inhaled a sufficient amount of smoke, held it in his lungs and then let it escape through his nostrils. "I'm sayin' man..." he was a bit reluctant about speaking on this specific issue, not because of fear but because he didn't want Jay-Roc to think he felt a certain way, but it needed to be addressed. "Roc I'ma keep it five hunit wit' you... niggas is sayin' you snitched." he side-eyed Jay-Roc to see his reaction. "I'm sayin'... I don't think you told; matter fact, I know you didn't tell, but this shit need to get cleared up."

Jay-Roc relaxed on the soft leather couch with a smirk on his face as he crossed one leg over the other and then touched the few hairs that were under his chin. He was about to speak when Babe Boy entered the lounge from the back room.

"Roc, what's good my nigga?"

Jay-Roc stood up and embraced his close friend. "Ain't shit homey, how you?"

Babe Boy was one out of a handful of people that Jay-Roc kept in contact with while doing his time. Before the indictment the two young men had done a few business ventures in the streets, but when Jay-Roc caught his case Babe Boy opted to drop his street ties and pursue a career in entertainment. At the start, Jay-Roc wasn't in agreement with what Babe Boy wanted to do; only because there were things that were done in the streets that needed to remain in the streets and in some cases lyrics have been used against those on trial, but after Babe Boy vowed to never speak the unspoken Jay-Roc used his pull in the game to orchestrate a power meeting with tops dogs from 3 major U.S distribution companies and within 72 hours Troy Carter, known to the world as Babe Boy was signing a six figure distribution deal.

"Did you get some sleep last night?" Babe boy took a seat on the couch.

"Barely... It's too quiet in that room. I'm use to niggas screamin' and hollerin' all night."

"Well you better get un-use to it homey... you in the world now and we them niggas on top." He tossed a set of keys and a red ticket with a number on it into Jay-Roc's lap.

"What's this?"

"The set is to the loft I got a few blocks from here; until you get your shit in order you can crash there if you want to, I don't ever go to that spot." Babe Boy received the blunt from Roland and took a deep drag of the potent smoke. "The ticket is for the Panamera parked in the lot across the street... oh yeah," he reached into his pants pocket, pulled out a black American Express card and placed it in Jay-Roc's lap. "Ain't no furniture in the spot... take yourself shoppin', get some ice... whatever. You home now my nigga." he reached over and gave Jay-Roc a pound. "I love you nigga."

The only thing Jay-Roc could do was smile. He cheesed so hard the corners of his mouth almost touched his ear lobes. "Mann... I don't even know what to say."

"You ain't gotta say nothin' my nigga. Live." He plucked the ash from the blunt into the ashtray. "This is the kinda shit you need to get used to." Babe Boy stood up and gestured for Jay-Roc to follow. "Somebody back here I want you to meet. Take ya' jacket of nigga, get comfortable... cool out; you too tensed."

Jay-Roc laughed and removed the jacket he was wearing.

"I see you was eatin' healthy in there huh?" Jay-Roc's frame was visible through the fitting thermal shirt he had on. "You almost starting to look as good as me."

Jay-Roc and Babe Boy shared a strong resemblance. Their skin tones were similar in color; both of them had a deep, brown mahogany complexion, full dark brown eyes and they stood well over six feet and weighed more than 200 pounds; Jay-Roc at 6'2, 240 and Babe Boy at 6'3, 265.

As they strolled down the corridor to the gold room studio Jay-Roc was racking his brain trying to figure out who he was about to meet. It could've been anybody. Maybe someone from his past that he hadn't seen since his departure; an old girlfriend or a homeboy, but that was unlikely because nearly all of his friends were either dead or in prison for life.

When Babe Boy opened the studio door Jay-Roc felt the bass in his chest from the loud music that was playing. He looked around in awe because he had never been on the inside of a recording studio.

A blonde haired white guy sat in a recliner chair in front of a huge mixing board tapping buttons and turning knobs. He made a gesture to someone that was standing behind the big glass window in front on him.

Babe Boy touched the white guy on his shoulder to get his attention. "Tell her to come out here Bill."

Bill pressed a button on the board and told whoever was inside the microphone booth to come out; seconds later the scent of a woman's perfume danced around Jay-Roc's nostrils. When he looked up to see the person who had come out, he immediately did a double take and then glanced over at Babe Boy and Bill.

Babe Boy grinned and formally introduced the two of them. "Mary this is my homey I been tellin' you about. Jay-Roc, meet Mary J. Blige."

Jay-Roc was so star struck that he couldn't open his mouth to speak. *Who didn't know Mary J Blige?* He thought.

He eyed her up and down and came to a swift conclusion that she looked much better in person than she did on television. Mary had gone from that young, wild tomboyish style hip hop look to over-the-top, star studded diva status. She was an icon and she was in the presence of a certified gangster.

Jay-Roc didn't want to come off like a groupie so he played it off by acting nonchalant and unmoved. "How you doin' Miss Blige?" he said.

Mary smiled and spoke back; she and Jay-Roc shook hands and she told Babe Boy that she had a show to do in Jersey later on and left five tickets in case they wanted to come through.

When she left out Jay-Roc tapped Babe Boy on his shoulder. "Tell me you hittin' that?"

"Nah... that's jus' business." He answered, trying to brush it off.

"Yeah right..." Jay-Roc laughed. "You see that ass Boy? Her shit is crazy! I know you hit that, you that nigga, you haaad to hit that."

Babe Boy was shaking his head. "She married Roc."

"What the fuck that mean? Mann... you know as well as I do how this industry is... shit, you know better than me 'cause you livin' it."

Babe Boy took a seat on the tufted, red linen chaise lounge that was pushed against the wall and slid a black, Louis Vuitton Damier duffle bag from underneath it. He unzipped it and dumped the contents onto the middle of the floor. "I definitely lived that life... ain't no lying about that. We done popped every bottle you can name in the club, drove every car that got four wheels... nigga, we used to go to the strip club and blow thirty racks. I was wildin'. Fuck it. I had went from sleepin' in a one bedroom apartment with seven muhfuckas, no lights and roach legs in the fridge to a three hunit thousand dollar custom built mansion on five acres of land. This is what it's about now." he fumbled through the stacks of money. "Two hunit and fifty stacks right here... all from three shows I did *last* week."

"Two fifty huh?" Jay-Roc quickly did the math. "So that's like... eighty three, eighty four stacks a show."

Babe Boy nodded his head. "Easy money Roc..."

Jay-Roc looked fixedly at the small mountain of money stacks lying at his feet. It had been years since he'd seen that much in one place at one time. On a few occasions he was able to coerce an old female friend to smuggle two or three bills in on a visit, but other than that the feeling of money had become something of foreign nature.

He bent down, picked up a stack of hundreds and flipped through them. Then he put the crisp, cut bills to his nose and drew in a deep breath. "I love the smell of new money..." he tossed the stack back into the pile. "I sat in that cell for ten years and not a minute went by that I didn't dream about this day. The day they would finally give me my freedom back." Jay-Roc went and took a seat next to Babe Boy on the chaise lounge. "When that judge sentenced me to all that time I thought it was over. I jus' knew I was never gon' see the streets again, but I realized I had to change my frame of mind and focus on the positive. I started reading a lot and studying those law books and in two thousand eight I got that letter that changed everything."

"Damn, that must have been crazy... But how did that shit come about... the appeal and everything?" Babe Boy questioned.

"The letter I got was from this kid in Jersey who was serving seventy five years for traffickin'. He was sayin' that he heard about my case and when he did some homework on it the same agents that were on my paperwork were on his and they were being investigated for tampering with evidence and supplyin' fake witnesses to guarantee convictions." Jay-Roc continued. "Long story short... the fed niggas went down and every case that had their names on it had to go back in front of a judge. So, honestly this dude who I had never come in contact with a day in my life helped me regain my freedom... along with what you did."

Roland was standing in the corner listening the entire time. His question had been answered. "Damn... so if he never wrote you that letter what would've happened?" he asked.

"Nothin'." Jay-Roc stood up. "Them crackers would'a let me rot in that muthafucka. After I got the letter I did my own homework and talked to a few old heads that told me how to go about filing the correct paperwork. It was a blessing that y'all blew up when y'all did because I didn't have anybody else I knew that could put up that kinda bread for an appeal lawyer. Shit worked out all across the board."

"Fuckin' right it worked out." Babe Boy added. "You on solid ground now homey... so what's your plan?"

Jay-Roc smirked. "You already know what time it is, we spoke on this."

"You still on that shit huh?" Babe Boy shook his head.

"Listen... let me take care of what I need to take care of and y'all niggas jus' keep bangin' them joints out. When it's time, then we'll connect." He gave Roland dap and went to Babe Boy to do the same.

"Be careful out there Roc..." Babe Boy whispered.

Before Jay-Roc left out the studio Babe Boy wrote down the address to the loft and told him where the car was parked. He exited the studio and walked across the street to the parking lot. After giving the attendant his ticket he waited three minutes and a gun metal colored Porsche Panamera pulled up beside him.

The parking attendant hopped out the driver's side. He was a short, chubby Mexican with a tattoo of the Virgin of Guadalupe on one side of his neck, shiny black hair that was combed back and a pair of black shades.

"Dope fuckin' ride holmes..." His accent was thick. He complimented and held the door open for Jay-Roc to enter. "Aye, not to be in your B.I or anything like that bro... but how much does something like this run?"

Jay-Roc was barely listening to what the attendant was saying because he was still in awe of the luxury vehicle in front of him.

"Vato?..."

Jay-Roc snapped out of his daze. "Oh, this?... it was a present from a friend. I don't know too much about cars, I jus' drive 'em."

"*Car?*" The attendant walked around to the back of the vehicle and studied it with his keen eye. "Holmes this ain't no car... V-8 engine, five hundred and fifty horses, six thousand RPM's and in three point five seconds this bitch is well over sixty miles per hour." he shook his head and waved his finger. "Nah holmes, this is a fuckin' machine."

Jay-Roc was impressed. "I see you know a thing or two about cars huh?"

"I love cars bro..." He went into his wallet, pulled out a card and handed it to Jay-Roc. "It's my life. Anything you need I can provide."

"Anything like what?"

"Secret stash boxes, bullet proof doors and windows, flip lights and license plates, oil slicks, smoke screens... machine guns... whatever you need vato I got you."

Jay-Roc looked down at the card in his hand. *Julio's Body Repair & Detailing* he mouthed to himself. "Okay... cool. I'ma give you a call and come by to check out some of your work."

"Sure holmes... I'm there every day except for Fridays. That's when I work here."

Jay-Roc got into the car and the attendant went back into his booth.

The plush leather sport seating hugged his body and immediately made him feel at ease as he adjusted the side and rearview mirrors. He hit the ignition button and you could almost hear nothing as the engine revved.

Jay-Roc placed his hands on the leather upholstered steering wheel and thought back to the last time he'd been in a car.

The loud sirens and flashing lights that trailed him on the of day of his arrest played in his head over and over again like it was merely twenty four hours ago. Federal agents cordoned off the highway only two exits from his destination and when they sprang from their vehicles they were waving guns and badges, screaming. *United States FBI! Don't move!*

When they placed the silver bracelets around his wrist and read his Miranda rights Jay-Roc was crying inside, but on the surface his emotions were as cold as an iceberg. He never made a statement, never implicated himself or anyone else and he stuck to his story of not knowing anything about drugs being in the car.

The day he blew trial and got sentenced to thirty five years, he stood behind that wooden rectangular desk in slacks and a Polo button up shirt with his hands cuffed behind his back. Jay-Roc was 100 feet from where the wrinkled face judge sat in her traditional robe and he kept his eyes focused directly on hers while she sentenced him to a lifetime.

He got startled when the car that pulled up behind him honked the horn. He put the Porsche in drive and slowly exited the parking lot. Traffic was flowing moderately when he pulled the $180,000 vehicle up to a stop light two blocks away. He hit the navigation screen and pressed the voice command button on the touchscreen.

Destination please? A female voice came through the speakers.

Jay-Roc looked up and the light turned green. He sat there for a moment and considered the plan he was about to put in motion. Going back to the hood was a must. There was unfinished business that needed to settled and little did his rivals know; he was coming to take his in blood. It was a plot that he'd been formulating for years and now it was time to execute.

He pressed the gas and the only thing he could do was smile.

"Bed-Stuy Brooklyn." he said.

CHAPTER THREE

"Deon lets go. You're gonna make mommy late for work." Malikah shouted.

She fastened her black slacks and snatched her nametag off the dresser. When she glanced at the clock she started moving a little faster. It was 10:12 and she was supposed to make it to work by 11:00, but with the daily delays of the New York City subways she knew for a fact that wouldn't be possible.

"Shit!" she cursed after stubbing her toe on the corner of the bed trying to find her other shoe.

"I'm ready!" Deon Jr. ran into the room. He was a spitting image of his father. Same eyes, nose and mouth, but he had his mother's complexion. "Mommy you alright?" he saw she was holding her foot with a painful look on her face.

"I'm okay. Where's your jacket?"

"Ahh ma... it's nice out." He replied.

"Nice my ass... Deon it's not summertime anymore, now go put a jacket on and meet me downstairs."

Deon pouted his lips and slowly walked away. He went into his room, got a jacket and went to the front door to wait on his mother.

Malikah rushed down the stairs fixing her hair in the process. She was agitated and the small toe on her left foot was throbbing. "Did you check the mailbox yesterday Deon?"

"Yesterday was Thanksgiving." He reminded.

With so much going on in her life it was becoming routine for Malikah to forget what day of the week it was or what month she was in.

She reached into her Prada shoulder bag and fumbled through the mess looking for the house keys. "You seen my keys Deon?" she dumped some of the contents onto the bottom step.

"No, but ma?"

"Where the hell are those keys?" she mumbled.

"Ma?" Deon tried to get her attention again.

"What boy!?"

His voice went low after she yelled at him. "Somebody's at the door."

When she lifted her head she saw a silhouette of a man standing at her door. "Who is it!? She yelled.

"Jayson."

"Who?" She went closer to the door and looked out the peep hole, but the person was standing too close for her to see. "If I can't see you I'm not opening this door."

"Malikah it's Jay-Roc!" He replied.

Jay-Roc? She thought.

"Uncle *Roc?*" Deon couldn't contain his excitement once he heard the name.

Malikah cautiously unlocked the door and peeked through the crack to make sure he was who he said he was. When she saw his smile there was no doubt in her mind that it was Jay-Roc.

"Wassup sis?" He cheesed.

"Uncle Roc!' Deon charged at him and wrapped his arms tight around his waist. It was the first time he'd gotten the chance to actually touch the man that had done so much for him in his father's absence.

"What up boy." Jay-Roc rubbed the top of his head and went to pick him up. "You gettin' big huh?" He held Deon Jr. in his arms like he was his own. He couldn't believe how much he resembled his father. It was like seeing King as a kid again. Even their mannerisms were identical.

As the years passed Jay-Roc understood that Malikah would have a hard time raising her little boy to be a man. Growing up he experienced the same troubles and was fortunate enough to make it through those rough conditions. If was up to him Deon Jr. was going to have some type of father figure in his life. So throughout his incarceration

Jay-Roc did his best to stay in contact with Malikah. They managed to speak once or twice a month and the first thing he would say is, *let me speak to lil man.*

Jay-Roc formed a kinship with Malikah and Deon Jr. through phone calls and letters. He promised himself that if he ever made it back to the world he would do whatever it took to make sure his best friend's loved ones didn't want for anything, and from the looks of things he had some work to do.

"What's this?" he asked, holding Deon in one arm and a yellow piece of paper in his opposite hand.

Malikah snatched the paper from his hand and crumbled it. "Another thirty day notice... It's bullshit. They'll take me to court, I'll give 'em some money and they'll send another one in sixty days." She sucked her teeth and tossed the balled up paper into the trash can.

Jay-Roc sensed it was more to than what she was telling. "You wanna sit and talk about it?" he asked.

"Look Jay-Roc..." She grabbed Deon from his arms. "I'm glad to see you. I'm happy that you're home and I hope you stay here, but right now isn't the best time. It's so much going on I can barely think."

"But this is why *I'm* here sis. I told you I wanna help. If there's anything I can do you need to let me know."

"Yes there is... move." She giggled. "I'm late for work."

"Mommy, can I get a bagel? I'm starving." Deon whined.

"Deon, I poured you a bowl of cereal. Why didn't you eat it?"

"Because the milk is stinky." He scrunched his face up.

"You tryna give lil' man some spoiled milk?" Jay-Roc laughed. "Since you're late lemme give you a ride to work."

"No thanks. Deon lets go." She started down the steps.

"But mommy..."

"Hold up sis." Jay-Roc blocked her path.

"Move boy." Malikah shoved him. "I gotta get him something to eat before he goes to the center."

"Aight, listen to this. You go head to work and have a great day and me and young King gon' kick it."

Malikah rolled her eyes and sighed. She disapproved of Jay-Roc calling Deon Jr. King. It stirred up too many past memories.

"I told you not to call him that Jay-Roc." She grabbed Deon's arm, pulled him close to her and stepped off down the street.

"Wait... Malikah!" Jay-Roc reached for her shoulder.

"No Jay-Roc... I asked you to stop calling him that."

"I don't see the problem. The boy needs to know who his father is Malikah."

"He does know who his father is *Jay-Roc*, but I don't need you reminding us every time we speak to you. I don't think you understand."

"*Understand?* You know what... go to work and me and lil' Deon gon' hangout."

Malikah didn't trust too many people around her son, but Jay-Roc was an exception. He was considered family to them and she knew he meant no harm in calling Deon Jr. by his father's name. It was just too much for her to stomach.

"Are you sure you can handle him?"

Jay-Roc looked at Deon and they smiled. "Of course I can. First thing we gon' do is get that nappy head cut."

Malikah checked her watch. "Shit! Alright... Jay-Roc make sure he gets something to eat and don't forget to bring him by the center, Ms. Baker is waiting on him." she rushed off down the block.

"Let's go lil' King... you wit' Uncle Roc today. What you want to eat... some McDonalds?"

Deon quickly nodded his head yes and they walked back up the block to where Jay-Roc's car was parked.

After eating Jay-Roc and Deon rode up Broadway and took in the sights of his old neighborhood. It had been more than ten years since he strolled these concrete blocks and although a decade had vanished most of what he remembered remained the same.

As he clenched the steering wheel his imagination took its course. He glanced over at Deon Jr. and envisioned him being his father and then a smile appeared on his face as he cruised up Broadway. He made a right on MacDonough Street, a left on Patchen and then another left onto Bainbridge where he pulled up and parked in front of his aunt's house. The only reason he was sure they still lived there was because he spotted his uncle's vintage, white 79' Ford Pinto parked in the driveway.

Damn, unc still got that car. Jay-Roc thought to himself as he and Deon walked to the front of the old house. He pulled the squeaky, broken down screen door open and rung the bell.

"Who da... he... hell ringin' at my gotdamn doe!?"

"It's me unc!" Jay-Roc answered.

"Me... wh... who?" He stuttered.

"Jay-Roc!"

"Two-Pac?

"It's Jayson unc!"

When the door came open Jay-Roc could barely hold his laughter.

"Unc, what's up!?"

Uncle Roy stood at the front door with a lit cigar in his mouth, a tank top on and a pair of tidy whiteys. "Boyyyy... di... didn't I send yo' ass ta' da' sto' lil' nigga?" his southern accent was heavy and he was squinting through his bifocals.

"Nah unc, that wasn't me. But I see ain't too much changed around here."

"Boy, I... I could'a sworn I sent yo' a... ass ta' da' sto'." He repeated.

"Unc, I jus' did ten years in federal prison."

49

Uncle Roy snatched his glasses off and stomped on the wooden floor. "Ten years!? Boy... you aint turn inta' one of dem switch-sidaz did ya?"

"Nah unc, I ain't wit that. Where's auntie?"

Jay-Roc's uncle Roy and Aunt Ruth had been residing at 264 Bainbridge Street since they migrated from Greenville, Alabama in the winter of 1970. They were amongst a handful of African Americans that actually owned property in this particular part of Brooklyn. Forty years ago the newlywed couple purchased the three bedroom house for less than $100,000 but with all the re-development in the surrounding areas the property value was nearly quadrupled.

"She in the kitchen where she 'posed to be... li... lil' nigga." Uncle Roy sneered.

"Yo unc, you gon' cut that lil' nigga shit out."

"Or *else?*" Uncle Roy stuck his chest out and pointed to his gun case. "Oh, th... tha... that's what I thought; you know I served in Nam lil' nigga."

Jay-Roc looked over to the gun case. "You still got them old ass guns unc?" he laughed because

Uncle Roy made it his business to remind everyone that came through the door that he served in the Vietnam War. "Them shits is like... eighty years old." He couldn't stop cracking up.

"But they work though." He blurted out and then inhaled a mouth full of smoke.

"Roy!" Ruth yelled from the kitchen. "Who you out there talking to?"

Aunt Ruth slid from the confines of the kitchen in her old faithful floral house gown and a pair of suede and wool moccasins. She was holding a spatula in one hand and a frying pan in the other. "Put that damn cigar out Roy. You see that baby standing there."

Uncle Roy turned to Deon and then to Jay-Roc. "Who this lil' na... nappy head nigga Jayson?" He let the smoke flow from his mouth. "Th... this yo' boy?"

"Nah unc, I ain't got no kids. This is lil' Deon."

"Lil' who?"

Jay-Roc ignored his senile uncle and went to greet his aunt. "Auntie wassup?"

Aunt Ruth had to train her aging eyes to get a glimpse of who was speaking. Her lips spread and her chubby cheeks lifted. "Oh my Lord!" she dashed back into the kitchen and placed the spatula and pan on the stovetop. "Is that you Jayson?"

"Yup, it's me auntie." He replied.

"I know I'm gettin' old. I can't even see." She opened her arms and they shared a tight warm hug. Aunt Ruth stepped back and got a good look at Jay-Roc. "Boy... you look jus' like yo' momma. I see ya' healthy... ya' took good care of ya' self Jayson. I'm glad ya' home."

A tear slowly crept down the side of her face, but Jay-Roc wiped it away with his hand and wrapped her in his arms again. "I love you auntie and I wanna say thank you for all those letters and money orders you sent me. It was days when I thought I wouldn't be able to make and I'd get that mail call and your words were the only thing that could bring me back to reality. I grew to rely on those words each month and you never once disappointed me. I appreciate that."

"Boy..." Aunt Ruth wiped her watery eyes. "You gon' make me start that cryin' again."

"Ruth! Where's my plate!?" Uncle Roy yelled.

"Roy shut up!" Her attention went to Deon Jr. "And who is this lil' handsome young man?"

"This is King's son." Jay-Roc said.

"Oh yeah?" Aunt Ruth remembered Deon because he would always come by and give her money to send to Jay-Roc when he was away. "You look jus' like yo' daddy boy. God bless his soul. It's always the good ones to go first..." she got lost in a moment for a second and then snapped out of it. "Well, I know ya' hungry. I got some grits, salmon, eggs and toast in there. You want me to fix y'all a plate?"

"No thanks auntie we jus' filled up on McDonalds."

"*McDonalds?* Boy, you better quit eatin' that poison. It don't do nothin' for ya' but make ya' fat n' lazy."

"I know auntie. When's the last time you saw my mother?"

"Hmph..." She rolled her eyes and sat a plate of food on the table. "Roy! Come get this food! I ain't seen yo' momma in two days, she out there somewhere. You know once she got a few dollars she don't come around here."

Uncle Roy was standing at the entrance to the kitchen listening to their conversation.

"Jayson." He said. "Yo' momma is a cr... cr... crack head. Ya' know that don't ya'?"

"Roy!" Aunt Ruth hit his chest with the back of her hand. "I told you stop sayin' that."

Uncle Roy took his seat at the kitchen table. "Goddamnit, it's the truth Ruth!" he slapped his knee and almost knocked his plate off the table laughing. "Everybody know it." his obnoxious shriek was annoying.

"Don't mind yo' uncle Jay-Roc, you know he ain't got it all upstairs."

"I got mo' den ya' think I got." He responded.

"Oh shut up n' eat Roy. Well, Jayson you need to come by and get a home cooked meal. I don't want you out there eatin' all that garbage."

54

"I am auntie." He and Deon walked to the front door. "I'ma stop by on Sunday. I know you chef'n up somethin' crazy."

"Okay." She said, waving goodbye. "Be safe out there Jayson."

Jay-Roc and Deon took a ride a few blocks over to his old stomping grounds on Putnam and Ralph. He parallel parked in front the bodega on the corner and saw a familiar face staring back at him.

"Wait right here." He told Deon as he exited the vehicle. "Hatman... wassup!?"

A short dark skinned African in a pair of blue jeans an army coat stood behind a table full of winter hats, scarfs and gloves. Finally recognizing who Jay-Roc was he rushed from behind the table. "Oh shit! Hatman!"

Meeko aka 'Hatman' was a neighborhood vendor who sold everything from tube socks to the latest Jordan's. He and Jay-Roc built a relationship more than twenty years ago when Meeko was running around in the streets hustling. Before Jay-Roc got arrested he and King gave Meeko the nickname

Hatman. It started out as a joke, but over the years it stuck.

"Some things never change huh?" Jay-Roc said. "You still in front of this store sellin' hats n' shit?"

"Not only am I selling hats in front of the store, but I own the store now Jay-Roc."

"Get the fuck outta here. You *own* it?"

"All mine Jay-Roc, shit... how long you been gone?" Meeko tried to think back to his last encounter with Jay-Roc.

"Ten joints."

"Damn... ten years Jay-Roc, that's a long time. I bought the store four years ago. Actually; it was exactly one year after they killed my boy King." He thought about it for a moment and then shook his head. "Damn I miss that dude."

Jay-Roc turned his head when he heard the car door open and then Deon jumped from the passenger seat. "Uncle Roc, can I get something to drink?"

"C'mere." Deon skipped over to where Jay-Roc and Meeko stood. "Hatman you know who this is?" he questioned, pointing at Deon Jr.

Meeko bent down and got a closer look. "I'll be damned... the legacy lives on." he shook Deon's hand. "Your father was a great friend of mine... him and your uncle Roc right here gave me the nickname Hatman. Hey, you know what Roc, I got something in the store that I've been holding onto for some years now. Gimme a second I'll be right back."

He dashed in the corner store and reappeared three minutes later holding a wrapped up brown paper bag. "The last time I saw King it was right where we standing. He pulled up right here." Meeko pointed to the street. "I don't know what kind of car he was driving, but it looked like a spaceship." he giggled. "He asked me to hold this for him and in two days someone was gonna come by and get it."

"What is it?" Jay-Roc asked.

"I never checked it Roc. I didn't want to know what was in it. I do know two days passed and he never called and then two weeks came and went, but he still never called. After two months I called him and said; you know I still got this bag. He said, 'What bag?" I said, the bag you dropped off two months ago. You told me somebody was coming to pick it up. And then he said, 'I don't know what bag you talkin' about but whatever's in it is yours.'" Meeko handed the bag to Jay-Roc. "I kept it stashed all this time hoping that I would see you again so I could give it you."

Jay-roc removed the rubber bands and unfolded the bag. When he looked inside and saw the contents he smiled "Hold your hands out." He said to Meeko.

"Holy shit Hatman!" Jay-roc dumped the bag in Meeko's hands until they were filled with rolls of money.

"Those are 5G stacks. He got that from me. I always rolled my money up like that." Jay-Roc paused for a second and painted the picture in his mind of King pulling up to the curb, hopping out and giving Meeko the bag. "Word... that's you though; he said keep it right?"

They counted ten rolls of five thousand dollars each.

Meeko quickly started tossing the money back into the bag. "I can't take this. I wouldn't feel right."

Jay-Roc thought about it. "Fuck it. Here King." he tossed the bag to Deon Jr. "Go get you ten juices."

Deon ran into the store and the two men followed.

Standing across the street next to the J train entrance was a slim kid with a black hoody, a black flight jacket, blue jeans and a pair of dark shades on. He tilted the pitch black specs and nodded his head to another kid that was standing by the fruit market about two hundred feet away. The slim kid knew who Deon Jr. was, but at this point he didn't care.

For the past few minutes they had been watching Meeko and Jay-Roc's exchange and their only concern was the goods that the brown bag contained.

An NYPD cruiser sat at the red light and as soon as it turned green, the two men made their move.

"Yo Hatman, I'ma check you out later. I'm 'bout to take lil' man over to the barbershop." Jay-Roc gave Meeko a pound and he and Deon walked out the store.

The slim kid and his accomplice watched Jay-Roc and Deon walk toward the parked car. Their eyes never left the bag that Deon Jr. was holding. It held fifty thousand dollars.

When Jay-Roc pressed the keypad the doors unlocked and the car started. Deon Jr. Jumped in on the passenger side and he got into the driver's seat. "You good?"

Deon nodded yes and then caught a glimpse of a man rapidly approaching his door through the side mirror. "Uncle Roc." he called out.

As soon as Jay-Roc turned his head, light skinned sprang from behind a van that was parked one car away. He grabbed for the door handle with his left hand and simultaneously squeezed the trigger of the black fifteen shot .40 caliber with his right hand. Fire shot from the nozzle and the sizzling lead jumped into the car barely grazing Jay-Roc's leg.

At the same time, his cohort pulled the passenger door open and attempted to snatch the bag of money from the five year olds hands, but Deon's clutch was too tight and the paper bag ripped open. Four of the money rolls fell into the car and the last six rolled into the street.

"Get down!" Jay-Roc reached over, pushed Deon's head down, swiftly threw the car in drive and mashed on the gas pedal. The screams from the burnt rubber spinning against the charred streets was ear piercing. "Keep ya' head down!" he shouted.

Three more shots came flying out the .40 caliber, two going astray and one crashing into the back windshield shattering the glass to bits and pieces.

Jay-Roc gripped the steering the wheel with one hand and kept the other on Deon as he maneuvered through the overflowing mid-day traffic. He floored the luxury vehicle all the way up Broadway until he came to Rockaway where he made the right and then a left onto Hull Street. He pulled over in front of 155; put the car in park and then looked at Deon. "Young King you alright?"

Deon brushed a few shards of glass from his lap and looked up at Jay-Roc. "Yeah uncle Roc, but they got some of the money." he replied.

CHAPTER FOUR

-THE NEXT NIGHT-

Torrential rain fall washed away littered debris on this windy, dampened Saturday evening. The lonesome streets were ridden of mulling pedestrians and the seldom passing cars had to dodge large pot holes that had been transformed into miniature pools of rain water.

A black Range Rover sport with dark tint slowed its tires and the driver pulled up to the corner of Ralph Avenue and Chauncey Street where Red and Butch were waiting in front of K&C grocery.

"Is that him?" Red asked, holding a large umbrella over Butch and himself.

"It better be him. I'm starting to get wet sittin' out here."

"Why the fuck did you bring me over here?" The female passenger of the Range rolled her eyes.

Rahmeek tapped a pinky nail sized portion of coke onto the back of his hand and pushed it up his nostril. "Listen... calm down alright." He snorted. "Lemme take care of this shit real quick and then we out. I know you hungry, I'm hungry too... shit, I wanna eat." he placed the top back onto the small vial of cocaine and stashed it.

"Well you need to hurry up 'cause you know I don't like being around this faggot ass nigga Butch."

Rahmeek pushed the door open. "I got you. Just chill..." he reached behind his seat and grabbed the umbrella that was lying on the floor. "Shit! It's comin' down out this muhfucka."

"Yeah, that's him. I can tell by those long ass dreads." Butch said to Red. "Yo Meek you got me out here for a hour waitin' on you. I fucked my new Timbs up in this rain."

"Fuck your Timbs Butch." Rahmeek walked around the front of the SUV. "I hope you called me out here to tell me you got that change you owe me."

"Nah... I mean... I got it; I jus' ain't got it all right now, but that ain't why I called you out here." Butch rolled his chair closer to the curb. "That nigga Jay-Roc is home."

Rahmeek turned and looked to Red and then back to Butch. He waited for an elaboration, but he said nothing. "So, what the fuck that mean?"

A deep thunder rumbled through the darkened sky and a sharp flash of white lightning illuminated the streets.

"Yo Red, hold the fuckin' umbrella... I'm gettin' wet." Butch demanded. He tried to show Rahmeek he still held some type of authority. "I'm sayin' that nigga Jay-Roc might want his revenge. You know King was his man n' shit."

"Ohhh... *that* Jay-Roc; well it seems like you got yourself a lil' problem. I could care less about a muhfuckin Jay-Roc. I ain't never seen that nigga a day in my life... don't know 'em and don't wanna know 'em."

Butch sucked his teeth and shook his head.

"What the fuck you suckin' your teeth for nigga, you got a problem?"

"I'm sayin—"

"You aint sayin' nothin'." He cut in. "Fuck is you scared of this nigga for?"

Butch chewed at his bottom lip. He didn't appreciate the way Rahmeek spoke to him. "I ain't scared of nobody. Only cowards live in fear. I'ma soldier."

"So man the fuck up and handle your business then. I shouldn't be gettin' no more calls concerning this Jay-Roc nigga."

"You right." Butch agreed.

"I know I'm right. I'm always right Butch." Rahmmek took a step and turned back. "Oh yeah..."

he remembered. "That lil' stunt you pulled in the projects on Thanksgiving; that shit was lame. I'm waitin' to hear from Alfredo now, it ain't lookin' too good for you."

"Fuck Alfredo. Tell that muhfucka to worry about keepin' the supply comin' and not what goes on in the streets of Brooklyn."

Rahmeek chuckled. "You got a slick tongue Butch." he walked around to the driver's side and got back into the truck. The passenger side window came down. "The only reason you still on these streets is because I allow you. Stay in your lane Butch." Rahmeek winked at him and peeled off.

"Fuck outta here nigga..." Butch mumbled as the vehicle pulled away.

"How you wanna handle this Butch?" Red was concerned. He knew Alfredo would cut their supply if he thought Butch would continue to be a problem.

"The only way I know how, Red." Butch touched the gun he had under the scarf on his lap and they crossed the street going back into the Brevoort Houses.

Rahmeek held the wheel and captained the Rover through the dark and rainy Brooklyn streets. "Why you ain't tell me that nigga Jay-Roc came home?" he said to his passenger.

"I was gonna tell you. You ain't gimme a chance."

"Stop lying Malikah. Don't gimme that bullshit."

She rolled her eyes, but looked straight ahead. "He came by yesterday to get Deon."

"He came *by?*" Rahmeek slammed on the brake and shot Malikah a crazy look. "Fuck you mean he came by?"

"I didn't know he was coming Rahmeek. He showed up at the door when I was leaving out for work."

"How the fuck he know where you stay at?"

Malikah got agitated with all the questions being asked. "He is Deon's godfather Rahmeek. I kept in contact while he was away... you know all this."

"I don't know shit."

She sucked her teeth. "Whatever... I need some money."

Rahmeek pulled over in front of a check cashing store. He put the car in park and scowled at Malikah. "Every time I turn around you talkin' 'bout you need some money. I jus' gave you money two days ago."

"Rahmeek I got bills." She stated. "Ain't nobody helping me with my son, all I ask you to do is help out with the rent sometimes. I got another fuckin' letter yesterday."

"Ya' son?" He put a confused look on. "I ain't that lil' nigga's father... and it ain't my fault you 'bout to get put out."

"Fuck you Rahmeek!" She tried to slap him but he caught her hand.

"Bitch!" He snatched a handful of her hair with his right hand, pulled the pistol from his pants with the left and shoved the barrel in her face. "I will fuckin' kill you! Get the fuck out my car!"

"Rahmeek please!" The tears poured down the side of her face, smearing her make-up. "Why you treat me like this? I love you..." she cried.

He reached over, opened the door and tried to shove her into the pouring rains. "Get the fuck out!" he screamed.

Her 140 pound frame slid off the plush leather and she fell onto the soaked concrete. "You fuckin' bastard!" she sobbed, Rahmeek closed the door and drove off without a second thought about his actions.

Cold rains drenched Malikah as she struggled to crawl back to her feet and when she looked up he was gone. The sniffles and faint cries of her misguided heart echoed throughout the listless night and the salty droplets that escaped the wells of her eyes got washed away by tears of another sort. Malikah couldn't understand how she had sacrificed so much; ultimately put her life on the line to be with this man and yet here she was again—abandoned, mistreated and blatantly disrespected. But over time she had become complacent with this type of behavior. She merely brushed it off or just dealt with it, sometimes she would act as if it never even happened. It was an issue of concern in every relationship prior to her and Deon getting together. He was probably the only man that truly did love her, but it didn't matter now because he was gone and the violent cycle of torment continued to plague her.

The physical and mental abuse had torn away at Malikah's soul and helped her identify love as the targeted enemy. She had it lined up in her scope like a proficient sniper ready to squeeze at the precise moment. Those four letters were the cause to everything that had gone wrong in her life. She hated love and love hated her. It was a mutual enmity.

When she finally rose to her feet she snatched her mini satchel off the wet ground and almost hit the pavement a second time because the heel on her cap toe pump had broken. "Shit!" she pulled the shoe off her foot and threw it at the gate on the check cashing store. Her hair was wet. Her make-up was smeared. Her clothes were soaked, and to make things a bit more difficult, her phone only had one bar of battery life.

She spotted temporary shelter from the hard rains underneath a small ledge in front of a hair salon adjacent to the check cashing store. So she rushed over and pulled her phone from the moistened purse on her shoulder. As soon as she pressed the button to power the phone up it blinked indicating that the battery was low and it would eventually shut off. "C'mon pleeeaaseee don't cut off on me now." She begged.

Quickly she scrolled through her extensive contact list and paused at a few of the names. She had friends and associates in all five boroughs, she could've reached out to anyone, but she didn't want their help, so she scrolled down to the J section; found his name and hit call.

"Hello?"

"Jay-Roc it's Malikah, can you come and get me?"

"What? Who is this?" He couldn't hear her voice over the downpour.

"It's MALIKAH!" she yelled.

"Malikah?"

"Yes! Can you come and get me!?"

"Where are you?"

She hobbled out to the curb and looked up at the street signs. "Flushing and Metropolitan." She read.

"What the fuck you doin' all the way out there!?" he asked.

"Listen... I'll explain when you get here jus—"

The phone died.

After waiting forty minutes more in the rain, a dark blue Chevy Malibu pulled to the curb and the horn sounded.

"You better hurry up before I pull off!" Jay-Roc yelled.

Malikah rushed to the car and got in. She was sodden from an hour of standing in the gushing rain.

"Damn... how long you been standin' out here?"

Malikah was so cold from the rain she was shivering and couldn't get the words out of her mouth, so she turned the heat up and placed her hands over the vents to try and warm up. Jay-Roc watched her, but stayed silent and just drove off. He wanted to inquire about what happened, but from the look on her face it just wasn't the right time. If the situation was that serious and she needed his assistance he was sure she would speak up.

They arrived at Malikah's brownstone on Putnam Avenue in less than thirty five minutes due to Jay-Roc pushing the Malibu to speeds exceeding seventy miles per hour. But the entire ride over nobody said a word and when Jay-Roc looked to his right Malikah was knocked out, sleeping like a baby.

"Yo..." He tapped her arm. "Malikah wake up." he used a little more force and her eyes popped open.

"We here?"

"Yeah."

"What time is it?" She cleared her eyes so she could see the time on the dashboard. "Oh shit it's eleven *thirty!* Jay-Roc can you give me a hand with Deon please?"

"Where is he?"

"Across the street at the babysitter,"

The hard rain slowed to a light drizzle as Jay-Roc carried Deon Jr. across the street in his arms. They managed to get him inside and in the bed without him waking up.

"Where's your bathroom Malikah?"

"Around this corner," she pointed. "First door to the right."

"This a nice joint." He complemented, finding his way around the pleasantly furnished three bedroom brownstone. He ran his hand along the marble counter top and looked around at the paintings on the walls. They looked to be worth some money, but Jay-Roc didn't know a thing about art. "You in to paintings n' shit huh?" he found the bathroom and entered.

"Not at all." She said, walking up the steps to the master bedroom. She peeled out of the soaking wet clothes that clung to her body and spoke loud enough so Jay-Roc could hear her. "Deon bought all those goddamn paintings. I was ready to throw 'em out."

"Throw em *out!?* Nah... don't do that. They look expensive."

"Jay-Roc, please..." she doubted that. "I think he bought those from the city... thirty fourth street or somethin' like that."

"Maybe, maybe not; I wouldn't throw 'em away though." Jay-Roc came from out the bathroom and went back into the kitchen. "Where you at!?" he shouted when he didn't see her.

"I'm upstairs. I had to get outta these clothes." Malikah wrapped a large white towel around her naked body. "I'm gonna get in the shower. There's some chicken salad in the refrigerator if you're hungry... some beers, Hennessy, juice; whatever you want. Make yourself at home. I'll be out in a minute."

Jay-Roc didn't know what to say, he hadn't planned on staying. "Ahh..." he checked the Audemar on his wrist. "I think I'ma go Malikah. I'll come check you out tomorrow."

76

"No!" She ran out to the top of the steps. "Don't leave. I need to talk to you. I'll be quick... Go ahead," she pointed to the living room. "Have a seat."

Jay-Roc was undecided on whether to stay or not, but because his last meal had been hours ago that chicken salad was starting to sound like music to his ears. He fixed himself a plate, poured a glass of water and sat at the dining table waiting for Malikah to come downstairs.

"Was it good?"

Jay-Roc jumped at the sound of her voice. "Oh shit. Don't scare me like that." he wiped his mouth with the napkin in his hand. "Yeah that was poppin' right there."

She smiled. "Thank you."

"You ain't make that." He joked.

"Yes I did." She snapped her fingers and rolled her eyes. "You better ask somebody."

They laughed and when Malikah walked around the counter and into the kitchen Jay-Roc couldn't help but to appreciate her well-built frame. She had a snug fitting pair of red shorts on, a grey sports bra and her long black hair was wrapped in a bun. Her skin was glowing and the lotion or body spray she wore filled the entire room with sweet arousing scent.

He tried his best not to stare at her alluring figure but it was becoming a complicated situation. Jay-roc hadn't been in the presence of a woman of Malikah's stature in a decade and his hormones were in a frenzy.

"You good?" She saw he was a bit tense. "Want some more?"

"Nah... I'm a'ight. Thank you."

Malikah opened a fresh bottle of Hennessy, poured herself a shot and took a seat at the table with Jay-Roc. "You know Ms. Baker called me the other day and said you didn't bring Deon by the center."

"That was my mistake. After we left the barbershop it slipped my mind." He lied. He sure wasn't about to tell her that he had her son in a shootout on Broadway in broad daylight. He just hoped Deon didn't say anything and from the looks of it, he hadn't. "How she doin' anyway?" he asked.

"She's good. She wants you to stop by and I told her you would."

Jay-Roc's eyebrows went up. "Oh you makin' decisions for me now?" he slid the chair back and got up to put the dishes in the sink. I'ma go by there tomorrow, but what about you?"

"What *about* me?"

"Cut it out Malikah. What happened tonight?"

She tossed the shot back and got up to get another one. "It's no big deal Jay-Roc. It was just a lil' misunderstanding between me and a friend. The conversation got a bit heated and I told him to pull over and let me out. My heel broke when I stepped off the curb."

He knew she wasn't telling the whole truth, but he wasn't about to go back and forth about it. One thing he did know about women was winning an argument against them like getting the national debt erased—it wasn't happening.

"Okay... as long as you're alright I guess everything is good. What you wanna talk to me about?"

Malikah guzzled her second shot and went for a third. "Well," she put her back against the refrigerator and held her glass while her mind wondered. "you know we've already spoke on the Deon situation and you know how I feel. Now; you may not agree with how I choose to deal with the circumstance but that doesn't give me the right to snap at you because you call Deon Jr. Young King." She sniffed the cognac and then took a sip. "I wanted to apologize to you in person for getting upset about that. I know I still have some things I need to work on and that's my main focus right now." She swirled the last bit of brown water around in the glass and then threw it back.

"You need to take it easy with that."

Malikah rolled her eyes. "This is routine for me. So what about you? What's your plan?"

"We talked about this over the phone." He replied.

"Noooo Jay-Roc. You have to let that go. Why would wanna jeopardize your freedom for some low life who has nothing to live for? You just came home."

"Listen... we not even gon' get in to all that right now."

"Hold on," she cut in. "Let me say something." Malikah took her seat at the table directly across from Jay-Roc. "Jay-Roc you don't owe Deon anything. I know you may feel like you do but really you don't."

"It ain—"

"Wait... let me finish. Deon had so much love for you it was crazy. He told me about how you were the one who had his back with that whole Butch situation back in the day. And how you got in trouble and went away for it; and how you introduced him to the street life... he definitely had a lot of respect for you. He always told me that."

"Deon was like my brother Malikah." Jay-Roc slowly dropped his head and bit down on his bottom lip. "I mean... we had our differences at times, but who doesn't? Like... for me to have to hear about what happened from some other nigga in prison and then I read about it in the paper... that was like some real heartbreakin' shit. I got so much anger and frustration built up that ain't no other way for me to release this shit without somebody gettin' hurt." he paused and ran a hand over the stubble on his face. "Somebody *gotta* get hurt 'cause I know for a fact he would've done it for me."

"But what is that gonna prove Jay-Roc? Going out there and bringing harm to someone is only gonna lead you right back to the hell you just came from."

Jay-Roc shook his head. He knew Malikah was telling was the truth, but he also knew the truth was a pain he didn't want to endure. He'd been dodging the truth his entire life. Why stop now?

"I'm not gon' sit here and go back n' forth wit' you over this Malikah." His whole attitude switched.

Malikah noticed the shift in his demeanor. "Okay... you're right, because it doesn't matter what I say anyway you're gonna go out there and do what you wanna do." She picked up the Hennessy bottle and poured her troubles into the balloon shaped cognac glass. "I do have something that I wanna give to you."

Jay-Roc's eyes went up. The last time someone said something like that, minutes later he was ducking hot lead. "What you talkin' about?"

Malikah strolled off and went back up the steps. "It's some of Deon's things!" she yelled. Five minutes later she returned with a small black safe box. "Here." she placed it on the table in front of him. *"Now where the hell did I put that key?"* she mumbled. "Oh... over here." she opened a drawer underneath the sink, fetched a small silver key out of it and tossed it on the table. "Open it."

Jay-Roc tapped his pointer finger on the table and eyed the box for a moment. "What's in there?" He inquired.

"Just open it Jay-Roc."

He picked the key up and looked at Malikah.

"Hurry up." she said.

He eased the key into the key hole, turned it until he heard a click and slightly lifted the top open. Immediately he recognized the scent. It was his favorite cologne. He pushed the top open all the way and the only thing he could do was stare at the contents.

"Remember that?" Malikah walked to the table, reached in the box and grabbed the chain with the crown pendant. "This thing is heavy." she placed the jewels on Jay-Roc's neck. "He wouldn't have wanted anybody but you to have this."

Jay-Roc glanced down at the diamond and ruby flooded King's crown lying on his chest. He remembered when Deon bought the chain. He grasped the crown pendant in his hand and ran his fingers over the solid gold crafting and flawless stones.

Malikah sensed Jay-Roc's emotions heighten just by the expression on his face. "There's something else in there too." she informed.

Jay-Roc reached into the box and pulled out a letter addressed to him, a small bottle of Versace Blue Jeans cologne and three Polaroid pictures. He put the letter to the side and sprayed a hint of the Versace cologne in the air. "This is still my favorite shit..." He sniffed, "I used to keep a bottle in the glove compartment for those spur of the moment episodes." He giggled. "One day King was like, *Yo, what's that cologne you be wearin'... that shit got all the females on you.* After I put him on, this is the only cologne he would buy." He placed the bottle back into the box and picked the pictures up. "Damn..." he held the Polaroid in his hand. It was of him and Deon standing in front of two BMW M3's; one red, the other one white. "Summer ninety-five... King's sixteenth birthday, I definitely remember this day. I called him early in the morning and surprised him wit' this joint." he went to the second picture. "Wow!" Jay-Roc couldn't believe Malikah had these pictures. "This was my twenty-first birthday party at the Tunnel in Manhattan. That night was crazy." The picture was of him and Deon standing in the V.I.P area of the club holding champagne bottles.

"Is that the night he got shot?" Malikah asked.

"Yup that was the night." A qualm feeling settled in the trench of his stomach as he recalled that night's events. He moved on to the last picture. "Who this?" he put the picture up so Malikah could see it.

"Oh... that's Rahmeek, Deon's friend."

"Okay, that's the kid Meek. I never had the chance to meet him." The picture had been taken six years ago so Jay-Roc didn't recognize Rahmeek as one of the dudes who robbed him the other day. His dreads were pinned up and he had dark shades on. "So when I'ma get to meet this dude, he still come around?"

Malikah hesitated. "Umm... yeah he still comes around."

"So what's his position? It's kinda obvious he ain't holdin' shit down," He was referring to the letter he saw the first day he came over. "You wouldn't be goin' through the shit you goin' through if he was."

"I'm not looking for a handout Jay-Roc. I can take care of myself."

"You're absolutely correct." He agreed to avoid an argument. "And I didn't mean it like that. I know you don't need a handout Malikah, but from the way it's lookin' some help wouldn't be too bad."

Malikah rolled her eyes. "I'm good."

"Whatever you say." He got up to leave. "I'ma take it back to the crib now, it's gettin' late."

Malikah followed Jay-Roc to the front door. "Well, if you don't get to meet him before Christmas I'm having a get together over here on Christmas day and he should show up. You can meet him then."

Jay-Roc didn't really have an urge to meet Rahmeek, he just wanted to see what the dude was about. "A'ight cool... so I'll call you sometime this week. I wanna come and scoop young Kin—oops..." he smiled. "I mean Deon."

"Good night Jay-Roc..." Malikah grinned. "I'll speak to you later."

The heavy rains had picked up again so Jay-Roc decided to jog out to where his rental car was parked. When he got in the vehicle he just sat behind the wheel in a cold silence. He peered up at himself in the rearview mirror and then looked down at the chain on his neck. The tears began to gather in his eyes and slowly drip down the side of his face. His sobs escalated and he sat there crying like a child who couldn't get what he wanted—like a big brother who had just experienced the loss of his little brother or a family member who recently had to part with a blood relative—he sat there, by himself, and cried.

The lost memories of the black safe box stirred up bottled emotions that were pinned down, but he could no longer suppress the pain. It all came out. Right there in the driver's seat.

CHAPTER FIVE

-SOUTH HAMPTON, NEW JERSEY-

"Yo Fredo I ain't lettin' nobody touch my hair." Rahmeek declared, yanking away from the guards.

"I invite you as a guest into my home and you tell me what you're *not* going to do? I would take that as disrespect if I wasn't in a good mood." Alfredo said. "Search 'em."

His two bodyguards grabbed Rahemek by the arms and continued their pat-down. "He's good boss." one said.

"Don't turn this in to a difficult situation Rahmeek. You're one fuck up away from being on my shit list."

Rahmeek sucked his teeth and then fixed his clothes after the guards searched him. "All I'm sayin' is... we been doin' business for a few years now. I understand you don't trust nobody, but damn... I'm ya' boy." He reached out to shake Alfredo's hand but was ignored.

Alfredo was in a good mood, but business was business and it always got handled accordingly. "Sit the fuck down." he hissed.

Rahmeek grilled the Mexican drug lord and then took a seat at the small glass table that faced a large Olympic sized indoor pool. "Nice view" he said, admiring the two beautiful naked females that were bouncing around in the water. "Nice tittes too." He laughed.

"Shut the fuck up Rahmeek! "Alfredo's voice was heavy. "I didn't call you down here to joke and hear about the latest hood news. There's a problem right now and it's yours... don't make it become mines."

Rahmeek ignored the threat. "May I?" he said, pointing to the humidor with cigars inside of it.

Alfredo sat directly across from him. "Be my guest." he slid the cigar cutter and lighter to the other side of the table. "Do I have to keep reminding you of why you're still breathing?" he poked his index finger in Rahmeek's face.

"Alfredo we been through this a thousand times. I know what you gon' say." He smelled the cigar and then chopped the tip off with the cutter.

"I don't think you do Mr. Tough Guy. Deon killed somebody who was like a brother to me. Prince and I... we struggled together; came up from nothing to something." Alfredo snapped his fingers and the two long haired women came from out the pool and over to the table. He stood up and whispered something in the taller ones ear and they exited. The men watched as their asses bounced with every step. They smiled.

"Them your bitches?" Rahmeek flicked the lighter and let the tip of the flame heat the fillers of the fine wrapped Cuban cigar.

"Don't concern yourself with that. Pay attention. I spared you your life Rahmeek... only because you agreed to kill Deon and make things a little easier for me, but you haven't gotten what I asked you to get and it's been five years."

"The bitch aint got the stone Fredo. I checked that whole house. I even got this bitch workin' at a sushi restaurant. She's broke, and if she had that stone she wouldn't be puttin' herself through the struggle that she's goin' through." Rahmeek sucked in a mouth full of smoke and exhaled.

"She has to have it!" Alfredo jumped up. "Maybe she doesn't know she has it?"

"How you so sure Deon took it?"

Alfredo pulled a cigarette from his pack and lit it. "I know he took it. I saw it the day before the murder. Prince put it in one of those barrels.

"Well I didn't see no stone."

"That's because you weren't looking for it you fucking asshole!" Alfredo's anger was rising and the sweat was beginning to build on his forehead. "That stone is worth fifty million dollars you piece of shit! You told me you would get it and now I'm really starting to think you were just bullshitting me."

Initially Rahmeek wasn't concerned with why Alfredo wanted the stone, but over the years the truth eventually surfaced and he figured out that

Alfredo had already planned on killing his friend Prince, but Deon beat him to it. When he found out about the murder Alfredo put a ransom of $100,000 on King's head. Being the goon he is Rahmeek took the bounty, but in turn paid Butch $10,000 and made it look like it was revenge from when Deon set him up to get stabbed.

Rahmeek then slithered his way into Malikah's life in hopes of her having the stone or at least knowing where it was. But that didn't look to be working and now he was sitting across the table from one of the most callous drug lords in the world. He kept his composure because he'd been in similar situations, but he also knew his time was running thin and it was either make a move or get moved on.

"I ain't bullshittin' you Fredo I jus' need a lil' more time."

"*Time?* I gave you time and you gave me nothing."

"Jus' a few more weeks and I promise I'll have that stone. Shit... I'ma put it in a box with a red ribbon on it jus' for you."

"You know promises are made to be broken right?" Alfredo laughed and then snapped his fingers again. The two females reentered the pool area, this time wearing silk black robes, carrying large black duffle bags.

Rahmeek squirmed but stayed in his seat. His eyes toured the room and his heart slightly sped up.

The women stopped when they got next to Alfredo and dropped the bags. He slid them over to the table where Rahmeek sat.

"A few trophies I picked up in the last week or two." He unzipped one of the bags and spread it open.

"What the fuck!!??" Rahmeek jumped in his seat and almost fell backwards.

Alfredo unzipped the second bag and cracked it open.

Rahmeek felt his lunch rumble in his gut and a strong sour taste filled his mouth. He struggled to keep it down but the faces of the decapitated human heads flashed one by one. He got down on his knees, held onto his stomach and vomit shot from his mouth like water out of a fire hose.

"And just in case you don't take me seriously..." Alfredo snapped his fingers a third time and when Rahmeek finally picked his head up he was looking down the nozzle of a chrome .9 millimeter Larkin and a 12 inch machete was touching his Adam's apple.

He was too afraid to say a word. His eyes widened and his breaths per second quadrupled instantly.

Alfredo stood over Rahmeek while the murderous females held him at bay. "I'm giving you until the new year. Either you have my stone or six pall bearers are gonna be carrying your headless body past your screaming mother. Show him amiga!"

She raised the long sharp blade, hacked a chunk of Rahmeek's dreads off and then tossed them in his lap.

Alfredo took the last pulls of his cigarette and stubbed it out in the ashtray. "Next time it'll be your fucking neck. Now get up and get the fuck outta my house."

"Dammnn vato! What happened?" Julio was amazed at the damage that had been done to the hundred thousand dollar vehicle.

Jay-Roc eased into the garage and put the car in park. "Got into a lil' fender bender as you can see."

"*A little?* Holmes... this is fucking wrecked." Julio snatched the half of cigarette from the bridge of his ear and lit it. "Those are bullet holes vato. You're lucky to be alive."

"Who you tellin'... listen, I like this car, but it ain't me. I need something more compact... with a lil' more kick to it."

"You want kick huh?" Julio grabbed a set of keys off the wall and dangled them in the air. "I think you're ready for the showroom."

He and Jay-Roc went into the back room of the garage and Julio slid a large curtain to the side revealing a freight elevator.

"What's this some secret society shit?" Jay-Roc joked. He went to step into the elevator, but Julio stopped him.

"Hol' up holmes… before we go down here, how much you got?"

Jay-Roc reached in his back pocket, pulled his wallet out and flashed the black card.

"After you," Julio followed him into the elevator.

They took it down 150 feet underground until it came to a stop in the pitch black. The temperature dropped 10-15 degrees and the air was dry and thin. Julio hit a button and the elevator's gate rose up. He hit another button and small LED lights brightened a corridor that lead to a steel door.

"We keep it cold down here so the rocks don't get damp and molded." Julio stepped out. "C'mon follow me." he said.

They walked thirty feet to the steel door where Julio entered a code onto the keypad that was on the wall.

"Y'all on some real James Bond shit down here."

"Cars are my life holmes, but some of the shit I like to do is illegal so me and my hermano had this showroom built exclusively for those who desire to have a few extras... if you know what I mean."

The keypad beeped three times and the steel door slowly opened. Julio stepped through with Jay-roc in tow.

"I think I know just what you might like."

After a few more steps down a second corridor they came to a wide open space that housed twenty-five custom designed luxury vehicles. Jay-Roc was in coupe heaven.

"You like what you see?" Julio saw his face light up.

"Definitely, but I need somethin' black."

Jay-Roc admired the assortment of vehicles. There were Benzes, BMW's, Ferrari's, Porsche's,

Maserati's, Lambo's and Bentley's; all custom colored and designed.

"Something black... something black?" Julio scrolled through his mental rolodex. "Oh... follow me back here." They trotted past a few more cars and stopped.

"Now this is what the fuck I'm talkin' about!" Jay-Roc was ecstatic over what he was seeing.

"Nice right?"

"Very nice." He replied. "What's the ticket?"

"Slow down vato I got you." Julio pressed the automatic start button on the remote key and the engine growled. "This is my baby right here. Two thousand eleven Lamborghini Murcielago. The dashboard says two twenty, but with the added turbo on this thing you can easily hit two seventy five... no problem."

"Damn... I didn't plan on goin' that fast."

"Hey holmes..." Julio shrugged his shoulders. "You never know. But besides the engine I kept this bitch stock on the interior." He pressed the door handle and it opened. "Very basic on the inside, real clean, crispy and comfortable; the ticket on this is three seventy five, but I can do it for three and a half straight up."

"Okay," Jay-Roc nodded. "that ain't too bad." He liked the car, but it wasn't exactly to his standards. "What about this joint?" he pointed to the 2011 black Porsche 911 that was five feet away.

Julio smiled. "Yeah, this is your style vato. This is the nine eleven super coupe. It may not be as fast as the Lambo, but she screams." he opened the door and gestured for Jay-Roc to get in. "See how she feels holmes."

Jay-Roc slid into the driver's seat and fixed his hands around the steering wheel. "This is mean... real mean."

"Check this out vato." Julio reached inside and placed his palm on the navigation screen. A small compartment opened up on the driver's side door containing a black and chrome rubber grip .357 snub nosed revolver. "It's one of the added incentives." he giggled.

"Ticket?" Jay-Roc asked.

"As is? One eighty, but for you vato... one and a half."

"Yeah..." Jay-Roc got relaxed in the seat and started adjusting the mirrors. "Let's get the paperwork done so I can get up outta here."

"Sure thing holmes."

Jay-Roc tossed the keys back to Julio and they zig-zagged their way through the maze of cars and into the shop office. Julio took his seat in the old school leather recliner that was behind the desk and Jay-Roc sat on the matching sofa that was directly in front of it.

After signing the necessary documents and going through all the proper procedures, it was a done deal. Julio stood up and reached across the desk to shake Jay-Roc's hand. "Pleasure doing business with you holmes."

"Likewise." He answered.

"Before you go I got something for you. Hold up." Julio left the office and returned with two cigars, two champagne glasses and a bottle of Perrier Jouet. "We gotta celebrate."

Jay-Roc agreed and stayed another hour smoking his cigar and sipping on fine champagne. He assumed the gesture was courtesy for doing good business, but what he hadn't known was that Julio fed him the half-truth the entire time. In fact, his only honest statement was his expression for his love of cars. Other than that everything was a lie and he told it just the way he'd been instructed to.

"So everything is good?" Jay-Roc tossed back the remains of his drink and stood to exit.

"Signed and sealed vato. I'ma slap this dealer's plate on there for you and you can drive right outta here."

Jay-Roc looked around for an exit big enough to fit a car through. "How I'm gettin' outta here?"

Julio winked and tapped Jay-Roc on his shoulder telling him to follow. They walked across the showroom and Julio pressed some buttons on a wall pad and the sound of a moving elevator could be heard. When it got to the bottom floor the doors opened and Jay-Roc could see it was bigger than the one they came down on.

"This is your ride up holmes. It'll take you right to Atlantic Avenue."

On his way out Jay-Roc noticed a tarp covering one of the cars. "Yo, what's up under there?"

Julio went to the car and peeled the protective cover off. "Two thousand eleven, cocaine white, Jaguar XKR 175 limited edition; engine custom, interior and exterior custom." He walked around the car and explained some of the features. "Bullet proof driver and passenger side paneling, bullet proof windows." He knocked on the glass with his knuckles. "These bad boys can stop a missile. We got the flip plates; flashing lights, oil slick, smoke screen, no flat tires and best of all... this is one of my favorites." He pressed something on a remote and two compact sized machine guns rose up from hidden compartments on the hood. "Fully automatic and they spit live rounds vato."

"What somethin' like that run?"

Julio put the cover back over the car. "Ain't for sale holmes."

"Everything got a price Julio. You know that."

"It belongs to someone already."

"And who might that be? He inquired.

"My old man..." Julio said, hitting the button to let the gate down. "Call me if you need anything."

The freight elevator brought Jay-Roc to ground level and when it opened he slowly drove in the directions of the arrows on the ground. He exited out an AVIS car rental garage at 237 Atlantic Avenue in downtown Brooklyn.

A pleasurable grin washed over his face as he carefully nudged his way into oncoming traffic, but as soon the light changed to green his cool smile transformed in to a bitter frown. He couldn't control his thoughts and at times he would think too much and end up reminiscing of past days. It angered him that his best friend wasn't around to cruise through Brooklyn with him in a new car like they had done many times before. It hurt—it hurt so much his body cringed at the thought of Butch's name and he was out there; running around like nothing happened, but he had no clue that shit was about to change.

CHAPTER SIX

A stagnant cloud of cigarette smoke lingered in the darkness that filled the medium sized room. With the shade down and the curtains pulled you would never know it was 3:15 in the afternoon and the sun was still glowing in the bright blue sky. Butch relaxed in his wheelchair wearing no shirt, a pair of True Religion jeans and brand new cheesy Timberlands. He took a sniff of the dope that was in the glassine baggie that he was holding and his eyes rolled in his head. His body jiggle, but the wicked smirk on his face let it be known that he was just fine, and so was the drug. He reached over and fumbled through the ashtray for his cigarette.

"So what the fuck is you tryna tell me Brenda?"

"Nigga read between the lines, I'm leaving ya' bum ass!"

"Leavin'!?" Butch rolled over to where Brenda sat on the bed. "Leavin' who?" He questioned.

"Butch get the fuck outta my face." She jumped up and tried to move him out the way. "Move!" but she couldn't get around the wheelchair.

Butch snatched the Ruger from his waistline and aimed it straight at Brenda's head. "Bitch I'll blow yo' muthafuckin' brains out. You know I ain't got nothin' to live for. Other than my momma... you the only person I love. I gave you everything, bitch!"

"Love?" Brenda twisted her neck. "Nigga the only thing you love is that dope. Fuck what you gave me, I'm not concerned wit' that material shit anymore. I'm pass that, none of that shit makes me."

"Bitch, I made you!"

"Fuck you Butch!" She pushed the gun out of her face and managed to put some distance between herself and Butch. "Look at you," she watched as his head slowly dropped to his chest. "Noddin' n' shit, you ain't nothin' but a fuckin' junkie."

The heroin was working at full swing now. Butch's bottom lip fell and a stream of saliva hung from the side of his mouth.

Brenda looked on in disgust. "Fuckin' dick can't even get hard... that's why I'm fuckin' the next nigga!" When she opened the door to leave the room, Red was coming in.

"What's up, where's Butch?"

"Move Red." Brenda pushed her way past and stormed out the house in a rage.

"What the fuck is wrong with her?" Red asked when he saw Butch sitting in his chair.

"Fuck that..." He nodded and bounced back up. "Bitch!"

"You always pissin' her off Butch. She gon' fuck around and leave yo' ass one day, watch." He laughed.

"Red shut the fuck up and close the door." Butch tossed his gun onto the bed and lit another cigarette. "How much we workin' wit'?"

"Six two." Red answered.

"Six two? Nah, that ain't enough."

"I know it ain't enough and Rahmeek comin' through here tomorrow to get that. What we gon' do?"

Butch sensed the fear in Red's vocal tone. "Don't worry about it, let me handle this. You jus' make sure he shows up here tomorrow at seven o' clock. Can you do that?"

Red said yes.

"Wassup wit' the Jay-Roc nigga?" Butch asked.

"No sign of him yet, a few people told me they saw him though."

"He's in Brooklyn and I want that nigga's head." He picked up the gun up off the bed and cocked it and looked at Red. "If you see that nigga its murder, death, kill on sight... ain't nothin' to talk about."

"Whatever you say Butch," Red brushed it off. He didn't feel the same way as Butch did towards Jay-Roc. As far as he was concerned, as long as Jay-Roc didn't fuck with him it wouldn't be a problem. "We got bigger issues to deal with other than worryin' about this nigga Jay-Roc."

"Worryin'?" Butch hit Red with the low eye. "Do I look like I'm muthafuckin' worried?" He held up the gun. "That nigga gon' pay for what he did to me, you hear me Red?" He made his voice louder because he knew Red was trying to ignore him. "Do you fuckin' hear me nigga? He put a seven inch blade in my back and paralyzed me for the rest of my life. I owe his ass. I owe his ass every muthafuckin' bullet that's in this clip and I guarantee you he gon' get 'em all, and if anybody... I mean anybody," he stared directly in Red's eyes. "Get in the way of that... they ass gon' get it too."

-THE NEXT DAY-

Malikah sighed in frustration. She'd been on her feet the entire day running back and forth from the kitchen to the dining area waiting on tables, serving patrons and getting cursed out. Twenty minutes before her shift ended she was asked to stay late. The only reason she agreed to do it was because she desperately needed the extra money for back rent that was due. She felt like she was working for the sole purpose to struggle and in the process her self-esteem was taking on a brutal beating. The only thing she really wanted to do was live comfortable and enjoy life with her precious son, but life had been far less enjoyable over the past few years and it didn't look to be getting better anytime soon.

"Malikah you got one! Table twelve!" Her co-worker yelled.

When she turned around she saw a scraggily haired Mexican dude in an egg shell colored suit sitting by himself at the table.

"Good evening sir, my name is Malikah and I'll be taking your order tonight. Would you like to start with something to drink?"

"Evening," he replied. "Yes, a red wine would be perfect, your choice." He closed the menu he was holding and handed it to her.

"Will you be getting an appetizer or straight to the main course?"

"Umm... I think I'll skip the appetizer and go for the smoked salmon with an order of coconut rice.

"Anything else?"

"That'll be it, thank you."

Malikah quickly jotted his order down on the small notepad she held and rushed back into the kitchen to give it to the chef. Walking out the kitchen she caught a glimpse of a co-worker waving at her from the other end of the restaurant. She couldn't make out the person's face she was standing with, but she could see that it was a man. Before making her way over there Malikah picked out a bottle of red wine and sent it with a waiter to table twelve.

"You're a hard person to find." Jay-Roc opened his arms to give Malikah a hug.

"Didn't know you were looking for me," she said. "How'd you find me?"

They embraced and she got a whiff of the Versace cologne he was wearing.

"I know a few people in a few places." Jay-Roc pulled his leather gloves off and stuffed them in his pocket. "This spot is a'ight. Why you didn't tell me about this?"

Malikah didn't answer because she was embarrassed, so she switched the topic. "It's cold out there ain't it? You want a table Jay-Roc?"

He caught the curveball she threw and just went along. "Yeah, I'm kinda hungry. I never had sushi though."

"First time for everything," She responded. "I'm sure you'll like it, follow me."

Malikah walked Jay-Roc to a table that was fifty feet from where the older Mexican dude sat. Having them close to each other made it easier for her to move back and forth when they asked for something.

Jay-Roc opened the menu and scanned through it. He screwed his face at a few of the ingredients that were in some of the dishes. "I don't know about this Malikah."

"Gimmie that," she took the menu from his hands. "Do you eat lobster?"

"Hell yeah."

"Alright," She closed the menu and pulled her pad from the pocket on her apron. "Try the lobster roll."

"What's in it?"

"Lobster salad, masago and avocado."

"Masago? What the fuck is that?"

"If I tell you're not gonna eat it."

"If you *don't* tell me I'm not gonna eat it." Jay-Roc laughed. "For real... what is it?"

"Okay," Malikah opened the menu and put it on the table to show him exactly what it was. "You see the orange/red stuff right there?" she pointed and Jay-Roc nodded. "That's the masago. It's the processed eggs of the capelin fish."

"Processed eggs?"

She slammed the menu shut. "Yeah, but trust me it's good. I wouldn't lie to you."

Jay-Roc huffed and his eyebrows jumped. "You sure about that?" He was joking, but Malikah took it literally. She was guilty and skittish, hoping he hadn't found out about her and Rahmeek.

"Am I sure?" She rolled her eyes. "Jay-Roc please... Don't go there. I don't need to lie to you or anybody else. I'm a single mother holdin' shit down the best way I can ain't nobody doing nothing for me, I do for myself; so who is there to lie to?" Malikah sucked her teeth, waved Jay-Roc off and stormed off to the kitchen. "I'll be back with your food." She mumbled. Halfway there she was stopped by the Mexican dude.

"Excuse me," He touched her arm. Her skin was soft. "Can I have the check please? It seems I can't stay as long as I thought."

"Yes, please sir can you give me just one minute and I'll be right with you." Malikah continued to the kitchen.

"But miss!"

"One minute sir, please!" She disappeared into the back.

Jay-Roc watched as the old Mexican dude grumbled with discontent. He looked like he was in a rush to leave, but the bill had to be squared away and he came across a bit impatient.

"Excuse me, miss!" He called out to another waitress, but she didn't hear him. When he stepped from behind the table Jay-Roc noticed he was dressed rather stylish. It was an eighties, Miami coke era type of swag and even in the dim lighting the diamonds in his ring were two stepping like Evander Holyfield on *Dancing with the Stars*. Jay-Roc made a mental note of everything. He also saw the custom made cowboy boots he was wearing. They were easily worth a couple thousand dollars.

Malikah burst through the kitchen doors holding a plate of food in one hand and a check book in the other. On her way to Jay-Roc's table she stopped at the Mexican dude and gave him the check book.

"Sir, I'm so sorry for the wait, it's been kinda busy today."

"No apology needed... Mah..." He couldn't pronounce her name.

"Malikah." She said.

"No apology needed Malikah; in fact I should be the one apologizing." He slipped a credit card into the check book and gave it back. "Thank you."

"You're welcome. I'll be right back with your card."

Malikah walked to Jay-Roc's table and literally dropped his plate in front of him.

"Damn... what did I do?" He watched her stroll off in the opposite direction. He shook his head, stared down at the plate of sushi in front of him, but then lifted his eyes when he felt someone looking at him.

"First time?

"Jay-Roc kept silent and nodded.

"I remember my first time trying sushi... been addicted ever since."

"What is this?" Jay-Roc pointed at something on the plate.

"The Mexican dude walked to Jay-Roc's table. "May I?" He pulled a chair out and sat directly across from him. "You got your soy sauce for dipping," he pointed and "Your wasabi for that extra twang in your roll. What you do is grab the chopsticks," he tried to guide Jay-Roc. "Pick up a little piece of the wasabi and put it on the roll and then dip it in the soy sauce and enjoy."

When Jay-Roc picked the chopsticks up he couldn't hold them correctly, but after a few minutes he got the hang of it and before Malikah came back with the Mexican dude's credit card Jay-Roc was nearly finished with his sushi.

Malikah was surprised to come back and see the Mexican dude sitting at Jay-Roc's table. "You guys know each other?"

They looked up at the same time but the Mexican dude answered. "No, I'm afraid we don't, excuse my rudeness." He extended his hand to Jay-Roc. "Alfredo... Alfredo Montega." He said, felling Jay-Roc's firm grip.

"Jayson Washington." he replied.

Introducing yourself by first and last name showed a sign of significance and importance. Jay-Roc picked that up quick.

"Here you go Mr. Montega, thank you." Malikah passed his card back to him.

"You're welcome." He slid his sleeve up to check the time and Jay-Roc caught a glimpse of the watch on his wrist.

"Jaeger LeCoultre... that's a nice watch."

Alfredo smiled, "You a watch man?"

Jay-Roc dabbed the corners of his mouth with the handkerchief he was holding. "Merely a connoisseur of the finer things life has to offer." He said.

"Well said." Alfredo straightened his suit jacket and put his shades on. "Good day." He said, exiting.

Jay-Roc stood up. "Yeah, I gotta get outta here too."

"What was that about?"Malikah inquired.

"He noticed I was a first timer and came over to give me some assistance." From where Jay-Roc stood he could see Alfredo walking past the front of the restaurant. "You saw that watch he had on?"

"Yeah, it was nice."

"Nice?" he giggled. "That watch cost four hundred thousand dollars."

"What!?" Malikah didn't believe it. "You ain't serious."

"Look it up." He sipped the last of his water. "Listen, come with me outside for a second."

"Jay-Roc I'm working."

He looked around. "Ain't nobody in this muhfucka."

"A'ight." She laughed. "Hold on, I'll be right back."

When she came back they left out the restaurant and went up the block to Jay-Roc's car.

"This is your car?"

"Yup," He reached in the backseat and snatched his Gucci bag. "Jus' got it the other day, here." He passed Malikah the bag and told her to open it.

"What's this for?" She zipped the bag closed.

"It belonged to Deon, but now it belongs to you." He got in the driver's seat and started the car.

"Jay-Roc I don't want your handouts." She tried to give it back but he pulled off.

"I'll be by with the rest in a few days." He yelled out the window.

Before Jay-Roc made the right turn he spotted the white Jaguar from Julio's showroom and he saw Alfredo open the door and get in. He put it in the back of his mind to go see Julio in the next few days; Alfredo just may the person Jay-Roc needed to meet.

CHAPTER SEVEN

Jay-Roc could feel the bass from the speakers in his chest as he lounged in the V.I.P area of club perfections. The thick white smoke from the fog machine lingered in the air and the strong scent of perfume and cognac was evident.

Beautiful naked women of all colors breezed about the establishment working the floor exactly the way they were taught. Their eyes were keen to a potential trick waiting to be taken advantage of. It was routine. They had been trained to spot a plausible victim from across the room, but what they failed to realize was that some wolves come dressed in sheep clothing.

It was the first time Jay-Roc had been in a strip club in years, and his only reason for showing up was because Babe Boy was going to be performing his new hit single; *Make It Rain* and he honestly wanted his homeboy to be in attendance.

Waiters dressed in all black carrying ice buckets with bottles and sparklers were cautiously moving in and out the V.I.P area throughout the night.

Behind his black thousand-dollar Versace shades Jay-Roc kept a watchful eye of his surroundings and every few minutes he would have to whisper the same line into one of the girl's ear.

"Go find a trick... I ain't that nigga." He hated for his personal space to be invaded and a lap dance was surely out of the question.

"You enjoyin' yourself?" Roland asked. He was seated right next to Jay-Roc on the leather sofa. He tipped the Remy bottle to his lips and let the champagne cognac warm his young chest.

Jay-Roc nodded.

"It's some badd bitches in this joint tonight Roc." He watched as the girls sashayed by.

"If that's your definition of badd I guess so."

Roland side eyed Jay-Roc. "So she's not badd?" he pointed to a short haired Dominican female that walked past. She had tattoos covering her arm, nice sized D breast and a plentiful booty.

"She aight..." Jay-Roc replied. He wasn't too infatuated with the stripper lifestyle. He didn't understand how a woman could degrade herself by taking her clothes off for a few pennies.

Throughout the night various females approached Jay-Roc, some wanting to dance for him, others willing to do just about anything to get close to Babe Boy's entourage, but they were all politely dismissed.

After a stellar performance Babe Boy went on his way and Roland and Jay-Roc were heading out the club when Jay-Roc spotted one of the females that was inside dancing. She was the only one he considered worthy of his conversation.

"How long you plan on doing this?" He asked.

She looked around because she didn't think he was talking to her.

"Excuse me?" She looked him up and down.

"How long are you gonna continue to disgrace yourself by unveiling what God gave you to keep a secret?"

She sucked her teeth. "Nigga please... who the fuck are you?"

Roland was close by ear hustling. "Yo ma, watch your mouth when you talk to my peoples."

"Your people?"

"Yeah.. my people." He assured.

"Oh," her whole attitude changed once she found out he was with Roland and Babe Boy. "I didn't know. I thought you were one of these lame ass tricks."

"Me, a trick? Never that." Jay-Roc said. "I jus' wanted to know why is it that you do what you do? That's all."

"Because the bills need to be paid," She answered, "and this is fast, easy money. I'm also saving up to pay for school."

Jay-Roc checked her out from head to toe. She was dark skinned, average in height; about 5'7 with shoulder length dark brown hair. Her eyes were almond shaped and matched her hair color, her thighs were thick and her ass was big, round and soft. She definitely had the potential to be wifey material. He thought.

"So shakin' your ass for a few dollars is the only job you could find?"

"A few dollars?" She laughed. "No it's not the only job I could find, I actually have another job doing construction in the daytime."

Jay-Roc and Roland looked at each other. "Construction!?" they said on unison.

"Yes construction. I'm a heavy equipment operator." Her cheeks rose up.

"Oh yeah?" Roland grabbed his manhood. "I got some heavy equipment for yo' ass."

"Roland please... I'm not talking about toy Tonka trucks... I'm talking about the real thing." She seductively bit on her bottom lip and glanced in

Jay-Roc's direction. "Wassup with all the questions though?"

"Jus' asking." He said.

Brown skin slowed up and stopped next to a candy apple red Lexus 300 that was parked a few cars from where Jay-Roc's car was.

"You haven't asked me my name yet but you wanna know everything else about me. Where dey do dat??"

Jay-Roc couldn't hold his smile. She was right. "You're absolutely correct. I apologize..." he reached out to shake her hand. "Jayson Washington pleasure to meet you." he said.

"Jayson Washington," she mocked him. "Sorry... I'm Alana, nice to meet you."

Roland tapped Jay-Roc on the shoulder. "Yo I'll meet you at the car."

Jay-Roc tossed him the key. "Don't be fuckin' wit' my music either." he warned. "Now back to you."

Alana was reaching in her purse when the bright lights of a blue and cream Maybach 62 caused her to shield her eyes. The luxurious vehicle came to a complete stop right beside Jay-Roc.

The passenger stuck his head out the window. "Yo Brown what the fuck is up wit' you?" he called out.

Alana ignored him and continued to search for her keys.

"Alana!" He yelled. "You hear me fuckin' talkin' to you."

She was getting frustrated because she couldn't find her car keys. "What Henry!? I'm tired; I just got off work... I'm going home. What do you want?"

Jay-Roc took a few steps back when he heard the door pop open. It was obvious they knew each other and he wasn't about to get involved in their domestic dispute.

"What I want? Bitch, who you think you talkin' too?" He stepped out the passenger seat and approached Alana. "Since when you start talkin' to me like that?"

"Henry not tonight, I don't have time for this."

Henry looked over to Jay-Roc. "But you got time to talk to this nigga!?"

"Yo homey-"

"Don't homey me." Henry cut him off. "I don't know you nigga."

Jay-Roc chuckled. "You right. Alana I'll see you around." he turned to leave and the look in her eyes was begging him not to go. Something was wrong and if anything happened to her it would be on his conscience forever. But despite his gut feeling he continued walking towards his car. With each step he could hear Henry and Alana's argument getting more and more heated.

A silence fell over the pale dark sky and the soft breeze came to a halt. Jay-Roc stopped in his stride. His conscience wouldn't let him move any further but by the time he turned around it was too late.

"Bitch you fuckin' that nigga!?" Henry's weapon was already cocked and aimed in Alana's direction.

When the shot went off the entire parking lot got low.

Jay-Roc hurried back to his feet and his instinctive will to survive made him reach for the gun on his waistline, but when he looked up the Maybach's tires were screeching and they were peeling out the lot.

He could hear the faint moans and grievous cries coming from a wounded Alana as she lay crumpled on the cold cement with a hot bullet lodged in her abdomen.

Jay-Roc paced, he was hesitant in aiding the bleeding young lady. He didn't know her and if he walked away he'd probably never see her again. It wasn't his problem. "Shit!" he cursed and took a couple steps towards the red Lexus.

"Please... help me..." Alana's body was wedged between the bottom of her car and the ground. She held her wound tight with her right hand trying to stop the bleeding, but the blood was oozing through her fingers.

"Yo Roc come on! Let's go!" Roland heard the shot, waited to hear more and then backed the car up to where Jay-Roc stood.

Jay-Roc rushed over to Alana and tried to carefully pull her from underneath the car.

Roland yelled again. "Roc! Fuck that bitch we gotta get outta here!"

"Roland shut the fuck up! I'm not leavin' her like this." Jay-Roc's heart was racing. "Help me get her in the car!"

Despite wanting to press on the gas and put this whole situation in the rearview, Roland sprang from the driver's seat and went to help Jay-Roc as directed.

"Hol' up... lift her head up slowly." Jay- Roc instructed.

"Where's she hit at?"

"Her stomach you stupid muthafucka you see all that blood."

Roland looked down and saw the burgundy stain on Alana's white mink coat and his stomach turned. He almost dropped her.

"Get it together nigga! We gotta get her to a hospital immediately."

Alana's body caught a chill, her eyelids fluttered and she was trying to lick her lips because they had become extremely dry, but she could barely breathe.

Jay-Roc felt her quiver and saw her eyes roll to the back of her head. "Alana hold on baby... We gon' get you to a hospital."

She attempted to speak but her words were barely whispers.

Once they got her in the car Jay-Roc directed Roland on which route to take to get them to the nearest hospital.

"Make the right on twenty eighth and then jump on two seventy eight. We gettin' off at exit forty one." He explained. When Jay-Roc looked down at Alana her eyes were shut. His heart dropped to his feet. "Alana!" he patted her cheek with the palm of his hand and one eye came open. "Stay strong girl we gon' get you some help. Jus' hold on."

After getting off at exit 41 Roland made a right onto New York 25A and then a left onto Northern Blvd. His inexperienced driving skills caught the eye of a traffic officer who was idle at the intersection of Northern Blvd & 39th street.

The lights and sirens wailed less than a minute after they flew by at speeds reaching 80 plus miles per hour.

"Yo I think police is behind us!" Roland nervously checked the rearview mirror.

"Jus' keep driving! Fuck them!" Jay-Roc was holding Alana in his arms and her blood was all over his Louis Vuitton shirt and slacks, but that was the least of his concerns. If she died in his arms he would never be the same again.

Jay-Roc didn't deal with death in a reasonable fashion and since the untimely loss of his daughter and her mother, he'd been having problems getting past the fact that people close to him were gone and he was no longer able to touch or talk to them; and on top of that while he was away he got the depressing news of his best friend's murder which furthermore crushed his broken heart into a million tiny pieces.

"Yo, Roc they on our ass!" Roland cried.

"Stop worryin' about the fuckin' police and get us to the hospital!" Jay-Roc's anger was coming to life.

Roland focused on the road and tried to block out the blinding lights and screaming sirens in the distance. As he raced through the vacant streets he noticed the signs that were pointing him in the direction of the hospital.

When they pulled up to the hospital at Queens Plaza Roland quickly threw the car in park and hopped out to help Jay-Roc with Alana.

"Hurry up... Hold her up for a second." Jay-Roc remembered he had the gun on his waist. He ran over to the driver's side, placed his palm on the navigation screen and the stash spot opened up on the side of the door. He tossed the gun in and frantically made his way back to Alana and Roland.

Three NYPD police cars rushed the scene and the officers lunged from their patrol cars wielding handguns and badges. "NYPD! Get on the ground!"

Jay-Roc stopped when they reached the front entrance and let Roland escort Alana they rest of the way. He threw his hands to the sky and slowly bent to his knees.

Two blue suited officers with their weapons drawn approached Jay-Roc, cuffed him and pushed him into the back of a squad car.

CHAPTER EIGHT

"Yo Dice here come that nigga Meek," Bally called out to his partner after he saw the familiar Range Rover bend the corner.

Dice looked up, frantically snatched his money off the ground and departed the circle of gamblers that crowded the sidewalk.

When the Range pulled to the curb Rahmeek and his partner Loose hopped out and advanced towards the C-low game.

"What's in the bank?" Meek asked, reaching in the pocket of his Sergio Tacchini jumpsuit.

"Twenty-five hunit," Bally yelled. He shook the dice in his hand and then set the rules for the game.

"All bets down, everything good in my bank. If you can stack it in the crack you get paid. Let's go bitches!" He let them bounce in his palm while the bets were placed and then tossed the three ivory cubes at the wall. "Five, five, two!" he shouted once the dice stopped rolling.

"Let me get those..." Rahmeek dropped a stack of hundreds on the ground and bent down to pick the dice up. "I ain't shake these bitches in a minute." He blew into his hand and let the cubes smack against the cement wall and down to the concrete. He watched as the dice rolled over.

"No point!" Bally yelled, "You 'bout to ace to that duce... watch!"

"Yo shut the fuck up. You talk too much." Loose was standing beside Rahmeek dressed in his usual attire; all black everything. He wasn't big in size, but rest assured the gun in his pants was probably half the size of his leg and his intent was to use it.

Loose was deemed a wolf in what he calculated as the concrete jungle. He prayed on the weak, stole from the poor and the rich and had a high prejudice for authority figures. His resume consisted of two cop shootings, a string of armed robberies and various bodies throughout the borough of Brooklyn.

Being around Deon for so many years Rahmeek learned that when moving in the streets you always need at least one person to watch your back; he also came to learn that that person could eventually be the one to take your life, so he kept Loose close to him, but he watched him even closer.

The obnoxious banter and traditional shit talking came to a quiet when Loose spoke. He glanced at each set of eyes to let them know that he knew who they were.

Bally copped a plea, "I don't want no problems Loose."

"Let's get this money Loose fuck that." Rahmeek shook the dice again and let them fly from his fingertips. When they stopped and he saw what his point was he sucked his teeth. "No bet."

Bally's voice went high. "No bet? C'mon Meek you gon' do me like that? That's an ace."

Rahmeek looked at Loose and shrugged his shoulders.

Before the barrel of the gun was halfway out his pants Bally tried to run off, but Loose's aim was precise. He let him run a few feet and then lined him up.

The shot tore through his calf muscle, blew out the front of his shin and before he knew it he was on his stomach stretched across the pavement clawing at the cement with the tips of his fingers trying to get away.

Rahmeek raked the money up that was left on the ground after the rest of the dicers ran off and he walked over to Bally. "Where Dice at?"

Bally was squirming. "I don't know man..." he cried.

"Don't lie to me Bally. I jus' seen that nigga out here." Rahmeek snatched the pistol from his shoulder holster and cocked it.

"I ain't do nothin' man... please Meek." Bally begged.

"It ain't about nothin' you did Bally... It's them niggas you runnin' wit'... they the problem. You know I always had love for you; still do, it's jus' a fucked up situation." He shoved the barrel of the gun to the back of Bally's head. "Don't take this shit personal Bally." Rahmeek bit down on his lip, gripped the weapon and easily squeezed the trigger.

Bally's skull fragments and brain matter decorated the already filthy sidewalk and Rahmeek and Loose jumped back in the Range and drove off.

A stream of smoke escaped Red's nostrils as he exhaled and allowed the toxic nicotine to soothe his tense nerves. "You heard about Bally?"

Butch stopped counting the money in his hands and looked up. "Fuck you talkin' 'bout?"

"They hit him this afternoon at the dice game."

"What!?" Butch was livid. Bally and Dice were his go to men and they also brought in the highest weekly gross. "Where the fuck is Dice at?" he questioned.

Red sat back in the chair and took another drag of his cigarette. "I don't know, ain't heard from him."

"You ain't heard from him? Ain't you supposed to be in contact wit' these dudes on a daily basis?" Butch was aggravated.

"I can't keep track of everybody and everything Butch. I got my own shit I gotta worry about. If you wasn't shovin' that shit up your nose we wouldn't have these fuckin' problems."

Butch tilted his head lightly to the right and the left side of his top lip jumped. "Oh you better than me now huh Red?"

"It ain't got nothin' to do wit' that Butch, you slippin'... even Brenda said it."

"Now you talkin' to my wife about me, behind my back? That's some real sucka shit Red. I thought you was better than that. I thought we was cool?"

Red shook his head. "Yeah I thought so to, but sometimes best friends become strangers." he plucked the ashes onto the floor and reached into his inside pocket. "What's this Butch?" he placed a mini recorder on his lap and hit play.

"Yeah... Red's my man, but if he cross me... I'll do him jus' like I did Deon." The tape went silent.

Butch's eyes lit up. "That ain't me Red."

"That ain't you?" Red was disgusted with his lies. "I know your voice Butch."

"I mean..." He tried to explain. "That's my voice, but I ain't never said no shit like that. C'mon Red you know me."

"Nah... I thought I knew you Butch."

*****

Two days prior a couple federal agents gained access to Red's apartment in East New York and waited 3 hours for him to arrive. Red was surprised when he flicked his living room lights on and saw a blue-eyed white man comfortably lounging on his sofa.

"What the fuck is this!?" He went to reach for his waist.

"Move and I'll send your maggot ass right back to the essence."

He hadn't noticed the second agent standing in the shadows with his weapon already drawn.

"Have a seat Michael." The agent on the couch directed.

Red looked at both men and then saw a badge and a gun lying on his coffee table. They did resemble police officers.

He eased up and took a seat on his recliner in front of the television. "What you here for?"

"My name is agent Rotelli and I'm with the FBI." He sat up on the couch and Red got a good look at his face. He was a young guy, twenty-nine, maybe thirty with a blonde crew cut, pale skin and heavy bags under his eyes. "We had you guys on our radar for quite some time now Michael." He pulled out four pictures and placed them on the table.

Red turned his head in disgust at the sight of the gruesome photos. The first one was of a young girl who had been shot in the head and left on a living room floor. Two of them were of young boys gunned down in the street and the last one his eyes fell on was of Deon.

"Nasty right?"

"What the fuck do you want?" Red went to stand up but the other agent put his hand on his shoulder and pushed him back in the seat.

Agent Rotelli continued, "We know you had nothing to do with these murders, but we wanna put an end to your partner's reign and we want you to be the one to do it."

"Me?" Red was confused.

"Yeah you; if you don't do this now Michael," Agent Rotelli pushed the photo of Deon to the front. "It's gonna be you in the next picture... agent Goss play the tape."

Rotelli's partner pulled a mini recorder out his pocket and hit play.

"Yeah... Red's my man, but if he cross me... I'll do him jus' like I did Deon."

Immediately Red recognized the voice as being his longtime friend Butch, but why would he say something like that?

"So?" Red tried to brush it off as if it was nothing, but he couldn't believe what he'd just heard. "I've known Butch for a long time... He wouldn't do that."

"Oh yeah?" Agent Goss replied.

"Listen Red... You got a chance to make everything correct. It's on you. We gave you the evidence and now it's your turn to make a decision." Agent Rotelli got up from the sofa, picked his badge and gun up and got ready to exit. "I hope you make the right one. Oh yeah... check your mailbox."

Red stood dumbfounded in the middle of his living room thinking about the words he heard coming out of Butch's mouth on that tape. He glanced down at the horrid photos that were intentionally left by agent Rotelli and shook his head and then he looked over at the mini recorder lying on the end table. He picked it up and pressed play so he could hear it again hoping something would change, but the words were still there and it was a clear indication of how things would play out in the coming hours.

Agents Rotelli and Goss sat in the car outside Red's apartment building.

"You think he went for it?" Goss asked.

Rotelli laughed. "He ain't got a choice."

*****

The next thing that came out of Red's jacket had six lead rounds in it, black electrical tape on the handle and a rusty hammer.

"Red put that goddamn gun down." Butch tried to speak with authority.

"Not this time Butch..." He got up from the chair he was sitting in and stood over Butch while he sat stiff in his wheelchair. He had the pistol pointed directly at his temple. "I was down for you Butch. I had your back."

"Red, don't do this."

He pulled the chipped, rusted hammer back with his thumb and took a deep breath.

"They set this shit up Red... That tape is a fake!"

Red's palm was sweating as he gripped the old .32 revolver. "They told me you would say that."

"They?"

Red raised the weapon and smacked Butch on the side of his face with the small gun. On impact the pistol went off and the blow instantly opened up a gash on his cheekbone causing blood to squirt ten feet in the air.

"Where's the money Butch?"

"What money!?"

Red lifted the weapon again and struck Butch in the same spot on his face.

"I'ma ask you one more time... Where's the money at Butch?"

"It's in the safe." Butch was crying, holding his face while the blood was dripping down his neck. He pointed to the safe underneath the bed.

Red pulled the safe out. "Open it." he pushed Butch out his chair and he collapsed to the floor.

In less than a minute the safe was open and Red was digging out the contents.

Butch rolled over on his back with a face full of blood and watched Red leave out. "What about Rahmeek?"

Red tucked the gun back into his jacket and looked down at his struggling friend. "That's your problem now."

CHAPTER NINE

After spending almost 72 hours cooped up in a filthy, over-crowded holding cell in central booking Jay-Roc finally made it upstairs to see a judge.

The entire two-and-a-half days he thought about how easy it was to land in the same situation he'd just escaped and his gut was telling him that it was time to make a change in his lifestyle, but his pride wasn't allowing him to let go of what he knew best and that was the streets.

He was aggravated and in desperate need of a hot shower. His back was aching from going to sleep on a steel bench, his legs were cramped, his neck hurt and he was ready to beat up the tough guy five feet away from him who had been talking shit all night. But before getting his case called he patiently sat on a wooden bench along with six other men waiting to speak to an attorney.

Jay-Roc chose a legal aid lawyer because he expected the case to be nothing more than traffic violations, but the entire situation changed when a tall, mushroom crop, black haired white guy came over to talk to him.

"How you doing today? Mr. Washington?" He asked.

"Yeah... that's me." Jay-Roc raised his arms. His hands were in cuffs.

The lawyer approached Jay-Roc, pushed his reading glasses up to his eyes and read the charges that were on the piece of paper in front of him.

"Mr. Washington... you've been charged with more than a few violations. Let's see..." he bought the paper closer to his face. "you got speeding, reckless driving, failure to yield, passenger safety, passing improperly... and about two or three more, but this is the one that's gonna hurt you the most." He put the paper in Jay-Roc's face so he could read it.

"What? I don't see nothing."

The lawyer pointed it out, "Right there... criminal possession of a firearm."

Jay-Roc looked at the lawyer like he was crazy. "What!? Don't play wit' me."

"Mr. Washington this is far from a game. With your record you're looking at some serious time depending on how this plays out."

Jay-Roc dropped his head and then looked up at the 6'2 lawyer. "Time?" he shook his head. "I gave the United States federal prison system ten years of my life. Ten long muthafuck'n years... I'll be damned if they get another second outta me. I don't know nothin' about no gun."

"It says here that an officer Ryan searched the car and found a black .380 caliber handgun underneath the passenger seat in which defendant Washington was sitting before exiting the vehicle."

"That's a fuckin' lie!"

"I'm just reading what's on the paper sir."

"Fuck that piece of paper!"

The whole courtroom turned to see where the commotion was coming from.

"Well... we'll see how this goes as soon as the judge calls you."

Ten minutes later he stood when the judge called his name.

"The State of New York vs Jayson Washington."

He and his lawyer approached the bench.

"Mr. Washington you've been charged with various traffic violations. Has council informed you of these charges?"

"Yes your Honor." Jay-Roc said.

"Are you also aware that you've been charged with criminal possession of a firearm in the third degree?"

Instantly Roland popped in his head. It had to be his gun and the fucked up part was he had gotten away.

"Yes your honor, but can I say somethin'?"

The lawyer tried to stop him from talking, but Jay-Roc wasn't listening.

"Sure, go ahead."

"That's not my gun."

"Is that it?" The judge asked.

"Yes."

"So you're entering a plea of not guilty?"

"Yes."

She slammed the gavel down. "Bail set at one hundred thousand dollars."

Jay-Roc grilled the legal aid. "I need a real lawyer."

On his way back to the holding cells Jay-Roc saw Babe Boy and Malikah walk through the courtroom doors. He knew they were there to bail him out, but he still couldn't force a smile.

They went and spoke to the court clerk and she told them what they needed to do in order to post his bail and twenty minutes later Jay-Roc was stepping out the doors of One Police Plaza, a free man—again.

"Trouble seems to follow you everywhere you go huh?" Malikah was leaning against Babe Boy's Bentley coupe as she watched Jay-Roc walk down the pathway.

He sucked his teeth. "Where that nigga Roland?"

"He at the studio." Babe boy said. "What happened?"

Jay-Roc ignored his question and walked around the car to get in on the passenger side. "I need to change these clothes and go by the hospital at Queens Plaza real quick and then we can go by the studio."

Those were his last words. The entire ride to the hospital Jay-Roc was silent. He just stared out the windshield and prayed that Alana had survived the gunshot.

When they pulled up at the front entrance to the hospital Jay-Roc jumped out. "I'll be right back... wait here." he made his way through the front doors and over to the information desk. "Excuse me a friend of mines was shot two nights ago and I wanted to know her status."

The young white girl sitting behind the glass window pressed some buttons on the computer and said, "We got six gunshot victims in the last two days. Your friends name?"

"Alana."

She pressed a few more buttons and said, "Alana Higgins. Yes, she's doing just fine. Would you like to see her?"

"Yes please."

After a routine check of his ID she printed him a visitor's pass and gave him directions to Alana's room.

Jay-Roc tapped on the door and a female answered.

"Come in."

He pushed it open and walked into the eerily quiet room. The person staring back at him had a strong resemblance to Alana, but she looked a few years older.

"Excuse me, who are you?" She stood up out the chair she was sitting in.

"I'm sorry... my name is Jayson and I'm the one who helped Alana get to the hospital."

At the sound of Jay-Roc's distinctive voice Alana lifted her head from the pillow and tried to see where he was. She was hooked to various IV's and could barely speak but managed to whisper. "Jayson..."

"Oh... okay." The older woman walked over to him and gave him a hug. "Thank you for helping my baby. I don't know what I would have done if that nut would have killed her."

Damn that's her mother? Jay-Roc's mind was wondering. "I'm just glad she's okay." he replied. He took a few steps over to where Alana lay in the bed. "How you feeling?"

When she finally got to see him a half smile crept across her face. "Not bad," she mumbled.

"That's good. I jus' came to make sure you were alright." He looked into her eyes.

With all of her energy she raised her arm and touched his hand. "Thank you." He could almost hear nothing, but his eyes read her lips and he knew exactly what she said.

Jay-Roc couldn't stay long so he left his cell phone number with her mother and said he would be back in a day or two to check on her.

"Yo I ain't moving this car until you tell me what's going on." Babe Boy had the keys in his hand sitting back in the driver's seat when Jay-Roc got back into the vehicle.

"Take me to the studio."

"Oh you giving orders now?" He sat up in his seat. "Nah Roc... fuck that... tell me something."

Jay-Roc glanced at Malikah in the backseat and then grilled Babe Boy. "Did I ever question you when you told me you had something to do? Did I ever second guess any decisions you made throughout our time on the streets?"

Babe Boy's voice was low, almost a hum. "Nah..."

"A'ight then drive this muhfucka to the studio."

Twenty minutes later they were walking into *Chung King Studio* in downtown Manhattan. Jay-Roc and Malikah followed Babe Boy to the back room where Roland and two of his homeboys were listening to beats and writing music.

The music went low.

"Yo Roland let me talk to you for a minute." Jay-Roc stood at the entrance.

Roland was so high he hadn't acknowledged anybody enter the studio. "Oh shit... whaddup Roc." he laughed. "Y'all niggas scared the shit outta me. What's good?"

Jay-Roc gestured with his pointer finger. "Come out here."

Roland got up and walked into the corridor with Jay-Roc. Babe Boy, Malikah and Roland's two homeys stayed in the studio. At first what they were hearing was a regular conversation, but after a few minutes it turned in to a heated argument followed by a loud thud like somebody hit the floor.

All four of their heads turned at the same time. Roland's two homeys jumped up like they were going to help their friend, but Babe Boy ceased that.

"Yo mind your business you ain't got nothing to do with that." He looked at Malikah, "Please go see what that nigga doin'."

When Malikah stepped into the corridor she saw Roland stretched out on the hardwood floor and Jay-Roc standing there looking at his knuckles.

"What happened Jayson?"

"Lil' nigga left a gun in my fuckin' car!" He kicked Roland in his ribs with his size 12's.

Babe Boy eventually came out from the studio to see what was going on. When he saw Roland trying to get back to his feet he just shook his head. "What the fuck you do now Roland?"

Blood was leaking from his nose and the side of his mouth. He turned to Jay-Roc. "I'm sorry Roc. I swear to God I forgot about that shit."

Roland had been so drunk and high the night of the shooting that he really did forget that the gun was underneath the passenger seat.

"This nigga left a fuckin' gun in my car and now I gotta deal with this back and forth to court bullshit."

"*A gun?*" Babe Boy was surprised. "What the fuck you doin' wit' a gun Roland?"

"C'mon man... Don't act like you ain't from the same place I'm from. You know why I had the gun. Niggas in the streets is predators and I ain't gon' be nobody's prey."

"So what you gon' do... gun a nigga down and end up with twenty-five to life or worse case scenario... niggas start shooting back and pop your top off; then what?"

"Man... a nigga ain't worried about that shit Babe Boy. As long as I'm out here I'ma carry that thang wit' me... simple as that."

Jay-Roc listened to the young dude speak his peace. He didn't agree with him at all, but who was he to judge the next person, he had his own issues to deal with.

"All I wanna know is who was that nigga in the Maybach?"

"Maybach?" Babe Boy was lost. "What you talking about now?"

"This nigga know who I'm talkin' about." Jay-Roc pointed at Roland. "The big nigga that was in the club buyin' all the bottles n' shit."

Roland remembered. "Oh... that's Henry." he said.

Jay-Roc nodded. "Yeah that nigga, who the fuck is he?"

Babe Boy knew exactly who he was talking about. "What Henry had to do with this?"

"The nigga shot his bitch in the parking lot."

Babe Boy still didn't understand. "So what you got to do with that? That's their problem."

"I was right there Babe Boy. I was talkin' to the bitch and this nigga roll up beefin' n' shit, so I stepped off. Next thing I hear is the shot. He hit shorty in the stomach had her laid out in the street like a dead dog."

"Leave it alone Roc."

Jay-Roc eyed Babe Boy with a face full of displeasure.
"Fuck you mean leave it alone... you know this nigga?"

"Yeah I know him and I'm asking you to leave it alone."

Jay-Roc smiled. "Yeah, a'ight Babe Boy; you got that one, but if I see that nigga in the streets and he so much as look at me the wrong way I'ma end his ass."

CHAPTER TEN

-DECEMBER 23rd 2011-

Light snow flurries fell from the cloudy grey skies and the winter breeze rustled the dry leaves from the Fall seasons past.

It was two days before Christmas and yet the streets of Brooklyn were as empty as a dry well.

Rahmeek and his young goon Loose prepared themselves when they stepped off the elevator at the third floor in building 245 at the Brevoort projects in Bed-Stuy.

Both men were dressed in all black. Rahmeek had a tight hooded sweatshirt on with the traditional black ski mask and Loose rocked a black, wool turtle neck with a pair of dark brown pantyhose over his head.

Loose looked at Rahmeek and cocked back his trusty .45 caliber. "Knock on the door," he whispered.

Rahmeek tapped on the steel door two times and seconds later they heard a child's voice.

"Who is it?"

Rahmeek looked at Loose and pointed to the door next to the one he knocked on.

"You sure?"

Rahmeek nodded and Loose knocked on the door.

No answer.

Loose put his ear to the door. "Somebody's in there." he said. He backed up, knocked on the door again and they waited.

Movement inside the apartment was evident, so Rahmeek clenched his weapon firmly and stood to the side.

"Who is it?"

Loose nodded his head quickly when he heard a man's voice and pointed at the door.

It's Red. Open the door." Rahmeek tried to disguise his voice.

As soon as they heard the latch come off Loose kicked the door in and it slammed against Butch's numb legs.

"You know what we here for nigga." Loose's gun was damn near in Butch's mouth.

Butch didn't hesitate. "Red took the money Meek. He did some bullshit."

"Fuck that money Butch this shit is bigger than that."

"Yo Meek hurry up and shoot that nigga." Loose was in a rush for bloodshed.

"You covering your tracks huh Meek?" Butch knew he was about to die. It was no talking his way out of this one. "You know once Jay-Roc find out you had Deon killed he's gon' come for you."

"Fuck Jay-Roc!" Rahmeek aimed his weapon, squeezed the trigger and discharged three slugs through Butch's chest.

"C'mon holmes! What happened now?"

"Got a lil' blood on my seats." Jay-Roc said as he pulled the Porsche into Julio's shop.

After getting his car out the police impound he had to bring it by the shop for some detailing and a bug sweep.

"Vato, you and cars aren't a good match."

"Can you clean it up and check it for bugs?"

"Sure holmes. I can do anything you want."

"Julio can I ask you a question?"

"Wassup vato?"

"What line of work is your father in?"

The question surprised Julio. "I don't discuss family business holmes. Why you ask anyway?"

"Just curious. I know a man who drives a car like the one he has, has to have some type of business."

While Jay-Roc and Julio were talking the white Jaguar pulled into the shop.

"Now you can ask him yourself vato."

Alfredo and another man stepped from the exquisite vehicle. They both donned custom French tailored suits with solid colored ties, dark shiny shoes and Carerra aviator shades.

Alfredo tossed his car key to Julio. "Haven't we met before?" he asked Jay-Roc.

"Yes sir, in the sushi restaurant." Jay-Roc extended his arm. "Jayson Washington." he said.

"Yes Mr. Washington." Alfredo shook his hand and then removed his shades. "Jayson I would like you to meet my son Jose," he gestured to the passenger. "It seems you've met Julio already."

Jay-Roc reached out to shake Jose's hand and was met with an icy stare.

Alfredo chuckled. "Don't mind him, he's antisocial." He walked over to the Porsche and looked in. "This your car?"

"Yeah."

"Got some blood on the seats."

Jay-Roc kept his eye on Jose. He didn't know him, but already he didn't like him. It was something about his vibe that didn't feel right. "Yeah I know, had to help a friend out."

"You gotta be very critical of those who you consider your friends these days. You never know who's out to do you harm."

"You're absolutely correct Mr. Montega. My circle of friends has decreased in past few years. Everybody's not to be trusted."

"The word trust is only as powerful as you make it."

Julio returned from the back room carrying a black duffle bag. He placed the bag into the back seat of his father's car and went over to his brother.

"That's a fine piece of machinery you got there Mr. Montega, must have cost a grip."

"Grip?" Alfredo didn't understand.

"A lotta money Mr. Montega. I'm pretty sure you paid a pretty penny for her."

Alfredo smiled. "Mr. Washington if you're inquiring about my business endeavors I'm quite sure you have an idea of what's going on over here. You seem like a smart guy."

Jay-Roc didn't know what to say. Alfredo read him like a short novel—quick and easy.

"I didn't mean it like that... I jus'—"

"Don't worry about it." He reached in his jacket and pulled out a business card. "Here, take my card. Give me a call after the holidays and we'll sit down and talk."

Jay-Roc took the card and glanced at it. "That's perfect. "he said, placing it in his wallet. "I'm sure we'll have a lot to discuss."

Alfredo checked his wrist watch. "It seems I'm late as usual... I'll see you around Mr. Washington. Jose! Vamanos!"

"Hey vato," Julio was holding a set of car keys. "It's gonna be a day or two before I can get that out the seat. I got you a loaner out front." He threw Jay-Roc the keys. "Don't bring it back with bullet holes."

Jay-Roc almost smiled, but he saw Julio was dead serious.

"I'll take good care of her... don't worry."

———————

Alana gathered her things and got ready to leave the hospital. After what seemed like a month, but was only a week, she was ready to be released. Her gunshot wound wasn't as bad as they thought it was and it was starting to heal up faster than expected.

Her mother helped her get her coat on and they were walking out the door when someone knocked.

"See, I told you he would show up, how you doing Jayson?"

Alana barely let him get into the room before she threw herself into his arms. She had a new found respect for Jay-Roc. He may have been hard as stone on the outside, but inside he had the heart of a saint.

"Wassup Alana." He hugged her so tight he felt her heart beat. "I'm doing jus' fine Miss Higgins, and yourself?"

"Just glad my baby is getting out of this hospital. I don't like these places." She said. "Alana you ready?"

"Yes mom. I'm gonna ride with Jayson."

"You sure? Is that alright with you Jayson?"

"Of course it is Miss Higgins. I'll make sure she gets home safe."

Jay-Roc escorted Alana and her mother out to the hospital parking lot and he and Alana got into the Benz truck that Julio loaned him until his car was finished. Before pulling off he looked over to Alana as she quietly stared out the window.

"What you over there thinking about?"

At the sound of his voice she turned her head and no sooner a tear raced down her chocolate cheek. Jay-Roc touched her face and wiped it away.

"Why you crying?"

"I don't know Jayson..." She broke down and now the tears were spilling by the dozens. "How am I gonna pay you back for saving my life? I owe you so much."

"Alana I did what I did because that was the right thing to do." Jay-Roc half smiled. "That was one of the few times that I did do the right thing. You don't owe me anything and I don't want you to ever feel like you do." He lifted her chin with his hand. "You hear me?"

She nodded and brushed the salty tears from her face, "Now what?"

"Now you got a choice to make, either you're gonna continue doing what you been doing or you gon' take this experience for what it is... which is a lesson, and make a change in your lifestyle. You ain't got no dreams? You never wanted to become something great when you were younger?"

"Everybody has dreams Jayson," her voice was soft and low.

"Yeah, but everybody doesn't get to live out their dreams. Not to be in your business or anything, but judging from what I've seen, I'm sure you got some paper stashed away somewhere. That money ain't gon' do you no good if you in a casket buried six feet in the dirt. Sometimes you gotta sit back and figure out if the risk is worth the reward, because in this lifestyle it usually ain't."

Alana took a deep breath and exhaled. "You right about that," she paused and thought back to when she was a little girl growing up in Bayside Queens. "I always loved planes. When I was younger I would draw airplanes all day long and pretend to be a pilot," she laughed. "That's something I've always wanted to do... I wonder what it's like to fly an airplane fifty thousand feet in the air and know that you're the one in control."

"So you like airplanes?"

"Love 'em."

"Why don't you go to flight school or aviation school... whatever it is."

Alana giggled. "To be honest, when I first started dancing I had intentions on doing that, but you know... being around all the bullshit got me side tracked and I totally lost my drive for it, but till this day it's still my first love."

"Did you ever check in to it and see how much it cost and all that?"

"Well, one requirement is a degree which I have. The cost of tuition to a certified flight school is roughly forty-five to fifty thousand dollars. Anything else you wanna know?" she laughed.

"Yeah," Jay-Roc said. "Sisters, brothers, age...wassup?"

"I'm twenty-seven-years-old no brothers and no sisters." Alana turned in her seat. "That's a little bit about me so, what's your story?"

Jay-Roc let his head fall back on the headrest and got comfortable in his seat. "I'm a Brooklyn kid. The streets raised me and prison made me a man, ain't too much to my story."

"There's gotta be more to it than that." Alana was intrigued. "C'mon, don't be shy now."

Jay-Roc almost blushed. "Nothing else; that's it."

"I think you're fibbing." Alana gave him that eye. "But okay, I'll let you get away with it this time."

They shared a brief intimate moment before Jay-Roc put the key in the ignition. He realized how beautiful Alana was both inside and out and his feelings for her had tripled within moments. He felt completely comfortable in her presence and he sensed she felt the same way, but a relationship at this point in his life wouldn't coincide with what he had planned. True he preached some good shit, but Jay-Roc was very knowing of himself and what he was capable of doing. He was a street nigga and the only way he thought he knew how to prosper in life was to apply the street mentality to any and everything.

"You ready to ride wit' me?" He looked dead in her eyes and she held her stare without a blink.

"Let's do it."

CHAPTER ELEVEN

-CHRISTMAS DAY 2011-

Malikah yelled when she continued to hear the little footsteps on the hardwood floor. "Deon! Stop running around in this house! You're gonna break something." She was standing in the kitchen rinsing collard greens in the sink and frequently checking on the turkey in the oven.

The entire house was filled with the scrumptious aroma of the holiday's favorite entrees and Anthony Hamilton's soulful vocals flowed throughout the atmosphere serenading the guest.

Every Christmas for the past three years Malikah would put together a family and friends soiree and invite all the people closest to her.

Like every other year her older sister Rasheeda and her husband flew up from down south to help out, her Aunt Tammy and her two kids showed up and her other Aunt Nora came with her newborn baby girl.

While the children ran rampant through the well-furnished brownstone happy to see each other on another holiday vacation the women prepared the last portions of the night's dinner.

"Malikah, where do want these?" Nora asked. Her arms were filled with pie crust pans.

"You can put those on the counter Aunt Nora. Thanks." Malikah checked the clock on the wall above her head. "Damnit! Can someone please go to the liquor store before it closes. You know it's Christmas they're gonna close early."

Rasheeda replied, "It's only three thirty sis... we got time, someone's gonna go."

"I'll go."

A man's voice came from behind them and when Nora turned around she instantly reached for the set of steak knives on the counter top.

"Who are you and how the hell did you get in this house!?"

"Whoa! Hol' up old lady!"

"Old lady??"

"Uncle Meek!" Deon screamed when he saw him.

"Wait! Aunt Nora, that's Rahmeek," Malikah shouted.

Nora had a steak knife raised in the air like it was a samurai sword. "I don't care who he is Malikah he called me old... I got to cut him."

"Nora put that damn knife down you scaring the boy." Tammy said. "How you get in here?" she asked.

Malikah looked at Rahmeek and then at her family. She didn't want them to know he had a key because they would immediately know they were messing around and she knew they wouldn't accept it.

"I think I left the door open auntie," she lied. "Rahmeek that would be nice; come with me in the living room so I can give you the money."

As soon as they got out of eyes sight Malikah cursed him out. "What the fuck did I tell you about using that key. It's supposed to be for emergencies Rahmeek and this doesn't look like an emergency to me. You're gonna wind up getting us caught."

"*Us?* No... I'ma wind up gettin' you caught. I could care less. You're the one that's worried."

"Fuck you Rahmeek."

His reaction was swift and forceful. Before his whole name came out of her mouth his right hand was wrapped around her throat.

"Fuck *me?*" His jaw was tight and his teeth were clenched. "That's how you feel Malikah?"

"Rahmeek... stop." She barely got the words out and then she felt his hand touch her breast.

"Bitch shut up." His palm connected with the left side of her face. "Get the fuck in the bathroom." He pushed her into the half bathroom that was a few feet away from the kitchen.

Malikah was holding the side of her face trying to keep the tears from falling. "Please don't do this Rahmeek."

He was oblivious to her cries and continued tugging at her belt until it came loose. "Take them shits off," he ordered.

Malikah understood if she struggled it would only make the situation worse than it was. She glanced up at the mirror while she slowly pulled her pants down. Tears of pain dribbled down her precious face and splashed into the sink. It was then she realized how fucked up her life was and the only person to blame was herself. Her thoughts were juggled when Rahmeek snatched a handful of her hair and slammed the side of her face in to the bathroom mirror.

"Fuck *me?*" Rahmeek repeated. "Nah bitch... fuck you." He bent her over the sink and violently entered her vagina from behind.

Instead of fighting it Malikah tried to enjoy it. She pushed the heinous reality from her brain and focused her thoughts on more delightful visions. It was difficult, but this false perception allowed her to believe that she wasn't being raped.

She endured the unpleasant pain for a few minutes more and then he was done. "Now clean yourself up and next time watch your fuckin' mouth when you talk to me." He slapped her ass and left out the bathroom.

On his way out the house he bumped into Rasheeda looking for Malikah. "Rahmeek where did my sister go?" she asked.

He lied. "I think she went upstairs. I'm 'bout to run to the liquor store. You want somethin' in particular?"

Rasheeda glanced upstairs and then around to the kitchen area. "No... just whatever she told you to get."

"A'ight, I'll be back in a second." Rahmeek slammed the door behind him and left Rasheeda standing there.

When the bathroom door came open Rasheeda turned her head and was surprised to see Malilah walking out fixing her hair. Although she hadn't seen Rahmeek come out the bathroom she assumed that's where he had come from since he wasn't in the kitchen when she looked.

"I was looking for you sis. Rahmeek told me you were upstairs."

Malikah went along with the lie. "Oh... I was upstairs a minute ago, but there's no more toilet paper up there so had to use this bathroom."

"Oh... okay." Rasheeda never imagined her sister wouldn't be honest. "Well, I put the collard greens on and took the turkey out the oven. You need me to do anything else?"

"No. Everything should be good. Now I'm just waiting on a few more people to show up but that's it."

"Umm..." Rasheeda licked her lips and batted her eyelashes. "I heard from a little birdie that Deon's friend Jay-Roc came home, where his sexy ass at?"

"Rasheeda don't start." Malikah turned to walk off, but her sister grabbed her shoulder and it made her jump.

"Girl... what's wrong with you? Why you so tensed? Loosen up... and call Jay-Roc's fine ass over here." Rasheeda burst out in laughter as they walked back into the kitchen.

———————

Scattered snow flurries fell like feathers from the skies above and for a minute it almost felt like Christmas as Jay-Roc pulled the keys from the ignition after he parallel parked in front of 685 Jefferson Avenue. Three young dudes all dressed in dark clothes loitered on the steps drinking forty ounces and smoking cigarettes. When he hopped out the truck the one at the bottom of the steps stood up.

The kid grilled Jay-Roc from the time his foot touched the cement until the time he was standing face to face with him.

Jay-Roc spoke first. "Whaddup?" He tried to say it in the calmest manner.

"Fuck you mean whaddup nigga, you know me?" The kid went to reach for his waist but his homeboy stopped him.

"Yo Crakz chill... that's the homey."

Jay-Roc didn't want to, but he quickly took his eyes off the kid to see who was talking.

"Yo Boogie that's you?" He couldn't see clearly until the dude removed his hood.

"Yeah that's me nigga, whaddup?" Boogie stepped down the stairs and greeted Jay-Roc.

Boogie was a childhood friend of Jay-Roc and when they first got schooled to the hustle game they would pitch in, buy drugs together and sell them in front of this same building. It looked like Boogie's routine hadn't changed a bit.

"It's been a minute my nigga, how you? I couldn't see you wit' that fuckin' hoody on."

"Yeah..." Boogie kept looking up and down the block. "You know how it is Roc. Niggas beefn' n' shit. Alien niggas ain't allowed over here that's why I keep my shooters on hand."

"Yeah I feel you. Yo, Fat Man still up there?"

"Yup. Damn nigga, didn't you jus' do a dime? And you 'bout to go see Fat Man... on *Christmas?* Yeah, you back on your bullshit huh, Roc?" Boogie smirked.

"Sumptin' like that." Jay-Roc walked up the steps and into the building.

"Yo Roc!" Boogie called out. He caught up to Jay-Roc in the hallway. "You heard about Butch?"

Jay-Roc hadn't heard a thing. "Nah, what happened?"

"Niggas bodied son the other night; ran up in his crib over in Brevoort."

"Word?" Jay-Roc smiled, but he had wanted to do that himself. "Niggas know who did it?"

"Nah, nobody know nothin'," Boogie turned to leave out the building. "Fuck around your boy upstairs know who did it."

"Who that?"

"You'll see when you get up there." he said.

Jay-Roc took the steps to the second floor, knocked on Fat Man's door and then heard the familiar voice answer from inside.

"Who the fuck is it!?"

"It's me Fats!"

"Me who!?"

"Jay-Roc."

"Jay-Roc?"

A few seconds of silence bypassed and the door opened, but no one invited Jay-Roc in, so he cautiously pushed it open and peeked in. "Fat Man!?"

"Come in Jay-Roc. I'm in the kitchen."

When he rounded the corner Jay-Roc saw Fat Man with his back turned standing in front of the stove cooking.

"They told me you touched down a few weeks ago, so I knew it'd be a matter of time before you showed up at my door," The Fat Man turned around and faced Jay-Roc. "But goddamn... on Christmas Day?"

"Since when did the holidays stop a nigga from takin' care of his business Fat Man? Your gate open ain't it?"

"You know this gate stay open, everyday all day."

"My point exactly," Jay-Roc approached The Fat Man, shook his hand and then hugged him. "I see you still the same fat, fly, rich ass nigga."

Fat Man popped the collar on his red Forzieri silk dress shirt. "You know how I do Roc... but check this out..." he leaned in close and whispered in Jay-Roc's his ear. "My cousin Red in the back all nervous n' shit, I told him you wasn't gon' fuck wit' him. Do me that favor Jay- Roc."

"I ain't got no problem wit' that dude, it was his boy I wanted to see, but somebody got his ass before I did."

"Yeah, I heard about that; so what you lookin' for?"

"Somethin' nice Fat Man, you know the type of shit I like."

Fat Man left out the kitchen and walked to a room in the back of the apartment with Jay-Roc following. He removed a key that was on a necklace from around his neck and unlocked the door.

As soon as he pushed it open Red jumped up from the chair he sat in and stood on his feet once he saw Jay-Roc. "C'mon cuz... you gon' do me like *that*? I thought we was family?"

"Red shut the fuck up. Ain't nobody doin' nothin' to you." Fat Man went straight to the closet and pulled a sheet off a safe that was on the floor.

"Roc I ain't have nothin' to do wit' that shit." Red was scared to death.

Jay-Roc rolled up on him and stared him in his eyes. "You sure about that Red? I heard different."

It looked like Red was about to cry. "Man... I swear on everything I love Roc, I tried to tell him not to do it. He wouldn't listen to me."

"You know if I find out you lied to me I'm comin' straight to you."

"That's my word Roc," he made a cross in his chest with his hand and then kissed it up to God.

"May God strike me down right here. I ain't got no reason to lie."

"Yo man... Leave that nigga alone. Red, give me and Jay-Roc a second."

"A'ight cuz... I'll be in the living room." Red got up to leave and never once took his eyes off Jay-Roc until he was clearly out the door.

"Scary ass nigga..." Jay-Roc giggled. "So what's good, what you got over there?"

"Take your pick." Fat Man had three handgun boxes on the floor. He picked one up. "This first one here is a full-sized forty-five ACP it weighs about 39 ounces." He took the gun out the box and handed it to Jay-Roc.

"This shit is heavy."

"Yeah, old school style. Brown plastic grip, seven shot magazine."

"Seven shots?"

"Yeah..."

"Fuck outta here." Jay-Roc passed the gun back. "That shit is trash. Next."

Fat Man cut a swift eye in Jay-Roc's direction. "What I tell you 'bout disrespectin' my merchandise. We went through this shit before; don't make me kick you out my gate Jay-Roc."

"I'm sayin'... I'm spending money Fat Man. I got a right to pick n' choose."

"Jus' hurry up so we can get this over with."

"A'ight, what's that?" He pointed at the second box.

"This right here is a Beretta BU9 Nano; all black, nine millimeter..." He opened the box and pulled the gun out.

"What the fuck is that!?" Jay-Roc couldn't believe how small the gun was.

"I said it's a nano. Now do you want it or not?"

"Not! Next."

Fat Man gave him that look again. "I'ma fuck you up Roc... For real. You got me sweating and breathing all heavy n' shit... lemme sit down." He pushed Jay-Roc out the way and sat on the queen sized bed. "This last one..." He picked the box up and opened it. "This is the CZ seventy-five B, double action nine millimeter with the extended twenty round clip," he gave it to Jay-Roc.

"See..." Jay-Roc smiled. "Now this is more like it." He held the firearm in his hands and got a feel of the trigger. "You said twenty rounds?"

"Yup."

"Perfect. What I owe you?"

"Two grand."

"Stop playin' Fat Man."

"I'm not playin' Roc... this ain't ten years ago. It's almost two thousand and twelve homeboy... you better get yo' money up."

"Get my money up huh? You right... I can't even argue over that." Jay-Roc pulled a knot of cash from his jeans, counted out three thousand dollars and gave it to Fat Man. "Keep the change. I'ma see you later."

"A'ight man... be safe out there Roc. It's good to see a real nigga back on these streets."

Jay-Roc left out of Fat Man's apartment, exited the building and hopped back in the truck.

CHAPTER TWELVE

Back at Malikah's house the holiday festivities were getting underway. After a few more guests arrived the drinks started to flow and the music was keeping the vibe up.

"Was that the bell?" Nora asked, looking at Malikah.

"Yeah I think so. Can you get it for me?"

Nora went to the door to see who it was. "Who is it?" she didn't hear anyone at first, so she said it again. "Who is it?!"

"Jayson."

She turned and Malikah gave her the head nod to open the door.

"How you doing?" Nora greeted.

"Hey..." Jay-Roc looked around because for a moment he thought he was at the wrong house.

"You at the right place, bring your handsome self in here." Nora let him in. "I'm Malikah's Aunt Nora and you are?"

"Jayson, Malikah's friend and how you doing?"

"Fine, thank you. You can hang your coat in the closet right there and come and meet the other guests."

Jay-Roc turned to Malikah. She was standing in back of her aunt off to the far right. His face said save me.

"Aunt Nora can you fix me another drink... and bring Jayson one too." Malikah knew her aunt loved to play bartender, so she enticed her by asking for a refill.

Nora jumped at the chance to make drinks. "Oh, you know I got you. I'ma make it real strong too." she ran off to the kitchen.

"So what's up? Don't look like much of a party to me."

Malikah grabbed his arm. "Whatever Jay-Roc. C'mon let me introduce you to everyone."

While Jay-Roc was being introduced to Malikah's Aunt Tammy and her kids, Deon came flying around the corner.

"Uncle Roc! Wassup!" He ran over to him and dove into his arms. Deon always got excited when Jay-Roc came around and Malikah took notice of that early.

"Whaddup boy?" Jay-Roc patted his head.

"Uncle Meek is here, did you see him?" Deon beamed.

"Nah... Where he at?" Jay-Roc looked back at Malikah.

"Deon go play with your cousins." She dismissed him after the guilt hit her like right hook from Floyd Mayweather.

The doorbell rang.

"I hope this is him right here. We're running outta drinks." Malikah walked to the door and when she saw it was Rahmeek she opened it. "About time." She grabbed the two bags he carried in his hands. "Wassup Loose. What took you so long Rahmeek?"

Rahmeek removed his hat and he and Loose entered the apartment. "You know I had to scoop my man up."

Deon raced back out of the living room and was headed straight for Rahmeek.

"Uncle Meek!" He shouted.

At the sound of Rahmeek's name Jay-Roc turned around and a sudden feeling of anxiety filled his body. He eyed Rahmeek and then glanced at Loose; then back to Rahmeek. His gut wasn't lying. He hadn't seen the dudes faces who stuck him up, but his intuition was on high alert, warning him that something bad was about to happen and only a few seconds passed before he reacted.

"Jay-Roc no!" The two bags Malikah was holding crashed to the floor and liquor soaked the hardwood.

Jay-Roc had the nine millimeter off his waist, cocked and pointed at Rahmeek's face in the blink of an eye.

"Don't hesitate nigga." Loose had his gun drawn on Jay-Roc.

When the bottles hit the floor everybody from the living room got up to see what happened.

Jay-Roc looked down and saw Deon. He was scared. "Move Deon!"

"Jay-Roc, put the gun down please." Malikah begged.

"A'ight," Rahmeek put his hands up. "Everybody chill... Loose put that fuckin' gun away, it's kids in here." He was calm and unfazed like this was normal to him.

Loose wasn't listening. "Jus' gimme the word Meek; I'ma push this niggas shit back."

"Loose chill!" Rahmeek knew his shooter was ready to put in work.

Jay-Roc gripped the gun tight and moved closer. He hadn't said a word, but he was focused on Rahmeek's eyes.

Malikah's family and friends were all back in the living room shielding the kids from any potential danger.

"Easy playboy let's talk..." Rahmeek tried to reason.

"Fuck talkin' to this dude Meek... lemme *DO* this nigga!" Loose had nothing but blood in his eyes.

Jay-Roc paid no attention to him, but after he thought about Deon and the rest of the kids that were in the house, he made a decision.

"Walk nigga." He moved toward the door and ordered Rahmeek to go outside.

Jay-Roc tucked his pistol, followed Rahmeek out and slammed the door leaving Loose inside, but

Loose wasn't feeling that so he snatched the door open and went to step out which wasn't a good move.

Jay-Roc heard the door open and instantly felt threatened, so as soon as Loose crossed the threshold he turned and hit him under his ribs with a short, stiff right hand. Loose dropped the gun he was holding, stumbled back, and grabbed his stomach. A yellowish brown liquid trickled out the side of his mouth and he slowly collapsed to one knee.

"Yo Loose chill!" Rahmeek yelled.

Jay-Roc shifted his attention to Rahmeek and skipped down the front steps of the brownstone. He was ready to fight because if he couldn't shoot him, he would at least get the chance to put his hands on him.

"Put your hands up nigga at least make this shit a challenge." Jay-Roc was adamant in his advance. He had his hands up, chin tucked in and his feet were firmly planted.

Rahmeek hadn't had a fist fight in over ten years; his last one being a Golden Glove Championship bout.

He smirked and tossed his hands up. When Jay-Roc saw his foot work he knew he could fight, which wasn't something out of the norm for a young black kid from Brownsville.

Rahmeek had come up in the unforgiving, murderous streets of Brownsville Brooklyn fighting every day and the only reason he picked up a gun was because he grew tired of beating everybody up. After a while the losers were coming back with weapons, so the only way he could survive was to grip up.

Jay-Roc threw a jab, Rahmeek blocked it. Rahmeek threw a hook, Jay-Roc weaved it. They danced around for three minutes and neither one of them connected a blow.

From a far it looked like they were playing and that's just what Ms. Baker thought as she strolled up the block in route to Malikah's. "Boy what y'all doin' out here?" As she got closer she could see the looks on their faces and knew they were dead serious. "Y'all bet' not be out here fightin' n' carryin' on."

It wasn't until she spoke that they acknowledged she was even there. Jay-Roc stepped back and slowly let his hands fall to his side and Rahmeek did the same. They had enough respect for her to momentarily put their differences aside and come to a peaceful conclusion.

"I want mines nigga." Jay-Roc was tight lipped.

Rahmeek sucked his teeth. "I got you homie. That thirty is nothin'," he replied.

Ms. Baker broke the tension. "Are y'all goin' inside or y'all gon' stay out here and dance wit' each other?" She laughed and they all walked up the steps and went back into the house.

After a brief explanation and some apologizing the party was right back to where it was before the drama started. Jay-Roc met the rest of the guests and he and Rahmeek even talked for a few minutes. The only person still salty about what took place was Loose. He was sitting in the corner of the living room by himself throwing ice stares at Jay-Roc all night.

A few more of Malikah's co-workers showed up and they all continued to enjoy each other's company, relax and have a nice, filling Christmas dinner.

It was 9:39 when Malikah looked at the clock and a little too late for someone to be ringing the front door bell.

"Didn't we have enough drama in this house for one day already? Now who the hell is it?" Rasheeda was drunk and very talkative as she walked to the front door to open it.

"Special delivery!" A man shouted from the other side.

Rasheeda looked back at her sis. "Should I open it?" she whispered.

"Girl open the door and stop playing."

Rasheeda slowly undid the lock and pulled the door open. "I didn't know they delivered mail on Christmas." she said when she saw the mailman.

"Yes m'am, we do. I have a piece of mail here for a Mrs. Malikah Toure. Is that you?"

"No sir." Rasheeda swung the door wide open and pointed at Malikah. "That's her." she slurred, tipsy and off balance.

Malikah walked over, accepted the mail, signed for it and closed the door when the mailman left.

She held the letter in her hands and tried to make out the return address but it was smudged. For a minute she thought it said Guyana.

"Lemme see!" Rasheeda went to snatch the letter and almost fell."

"Rasheeda, go sit your drunk ass down. You do this every year. Tammy!" Malikah called to her aunt that always puts Rasheeda in her place when she starts to act up. "Come get your niece... she's drunk... as usual."

Malikah bought the letter into the living room so she could sit down and open it. She ripped the paper off the envelope and read the letter:

Dear Malikah,

You don't know me but my name is Akbar Toure and I'm Deon's younger brother. Me and my sister, Bibi would be honored if we could have the chance to meet you in person. We also wanted to know if you could bring Deon's ashes so they could be placed in the same shrine as his mother and father. No response is needed, but if you decide to make the trip please call us at this number.

1-594-555-9876

Thank you, your brother and sister... Akbar & Bibi

Malikah had to re-read the letter two or three times before it really soaked in.

"Oh my God, Jay-Roc look." She held up the letter.

Rahmeek looked up when she called Jay-Roc's name. He was upset she didn't call him.

Jay-Roc went over to where she sat and read the letter for himself.

"Yeah, I need a vacation..." he said. "Let's go."

Malikah looked at him like he was crazy. "Go where? Jay-Roc, I have to work; remember I have a job."

"What does the letter say Malikah?" Nora asked.

"It's from Deon's brother and sister. They want me to bring his ashes to Guyana so he can be with his mother and father."

"Really? You should go."

"Yeah, I think we should all go." Rahmeek butted in.

Jay-Roc looked at Rahmeek and then Malikah looked at both of them.

"I'm gonna lose my job messing with y'all..."

CHAPTER THIRTEEN

"Boy, what you mean you going to Guyana? You know how far that is?" Aunt Ruth couldn't believe what Jay-Roc was saying.

"It ain't that far auntie and plus this is Deon's brother and sister I'm goin' to see. He didn't even know he had more siblings."

Jay-Roc lounged on the couch next to his uncle Roy who was reading the morning paper. He stopped by to let them know that he was about to take a trip out the country.

"And what about court?" She caught him off guard with that one because he hadn't said anything about his arrest to anyone.

"How you find out about that?"

Uncle Roy dropped the paper, looked at Jay-Roc and slapped the back of his neck. "Boy... You kn... know she get all the latest gossip."

"Yo unc if you hit me again I'ma knock you out." Jay-Roc rubbed the back of his neck.

Uncle Roy turned his lip up and pointed to his gun case. "Boyyy..." he shook his head.

"Shut up Roy." Aunt Ruth got up and went over to the computer. She typed in a web address and scrolled through a few pictures. "Look, they got you on the third page Jayson."

Jay-Roc hopped off the couch and went to see what his aunt was talking about. "What the fuck!? Oh... excuse me auntie." he was looking at a picture of himself in handcuffs being put into a police car. "What is this?"

"One of those hip hop gossip blogs. I always go on here. People always makin' a fool of they selves. I saw this yesterday. Why didn't you tell me?"

Jay-Roc was in awe of what he was looking at. The website had pictures of him the night he got arrested; in cuffs being pushed into an unmarked police car, in the club before the shooting and they also had pictures of Alana dancing on a stage full of dollar bills.

The only people that came to mind were Babe Boy and Roland. They had to have something to do with this.

"I don't have to go back to court until February auntie. I'm good."

"Um hmm..." She cut her eye at him. "Well, you better be safe out there. And don't drink the water," she warned.

"Yeah..." Uncle Roy had to put in his two cents. "And stay yo ass fr... from 'round dem woods. Them goddamn jungles ain't no joke."

"Uncle Roy what you know about the jungles of Guyana?"

"The jungle is the jungle lil... lil nigga. One of dem goddamn snakes bite you in yo' ass you... you gon' learn. Oh yeah... you gon' learn."

"Whatever unc." Jay-Roc got up. "I'ma call you when I get there auntie." He walked to the front door. "Uncle Roy I think they towing your car."

Roy jumped up to look out the window and almost tripped in the process.

"Haaa... got cha!" Jay-Roc joked.

"Boyyy..." Uncle Roy limped to his gun case, but Jay-Roc was out the door. "I'ma put my boot in yo' ass next time ya' come 'round here lil' nigga." When he was mad his words came out clear; no stuttering.

Jay-Roc jumped in the truck and hit the highway going to Queens so he could see Alana before he left. He had a whole three hours before his flight departed and she wanted to see him before he went on his trip.

He was lucky enough to find a parking spot not too far from the address that she texted him and when he got upstairs to the apartment he was surprised.

It was a one bedroom co-op in Rego Park, Queens that her mother owned and was renting out. From the looks of the outside of the building Jay -Roc didn't expect to walk into such a modernized, well furnished apartment, but it was much nicer than he assumed.

The floors were genuine walnut and cherry wood and the ceilings were at least 15 feet high.

"You stay here all by yourself huh?" Jay-Roc relaxed on the fine, French ivory linen sofa chair.

"Not all the time." Alana answered. She was pouring herself a glass of champagne at the mini bar in the far left corner of the apartment. "My younger brother stays here with me sometimes. He goes to school at Christ the King in Middle Village."

"Wait..." Jay-Roc thought on something. He remembered when the receptionist at the hospital said Alana's last name. "Your brother is Bobby Higgins?"

"Yup. That's him."

"Oh shit... that's wassup, that lil' nigga nice. If they was still lettin' kids in the NBA straight from high school he would definitely be in the league."

209

Jay-Roc had read about Alana's little brother in the paper several times. He was the best shooting guard in the country and well on his way to the NBA if he continued on the right path.

"Yeah, as long as he keep his head in those books and not these nasty ass bitches he'll be fine." She said. "You want a drink?"

"No thank you, I'm alright." Jay-Roc got up and walked over to the big window. It stretched from the floor to the ceiling and overlooked the city. "This is a nice view you got here."

"Thank you. You should see it at night. It's beautiful."

"I'm sure it is. So what's this big surprise you was talkin' about on the phone?"

"Oh... hold on." Alana ran to the back room and came right back holding a small red bag. "Merry Christmas!" she handed it to him.

"Aww, you got me a gift?"

"Yup." Alana grabbed his hand and brought him over to the sofa. "I know you said you don't really celebrate Christmas, but when I saw this, I thought of you. C'mon open it."

Jay-Roc pulled a small box out the bag and ripped the wrapping paper off. When he opened the box the light coming in from the window hit the diamonds and made them glisten.

"Damn this nice."

Alana reached over and took the ring out the box. "Let me see if it fits you." She grabbed Jay-Roc's hand and slid the 18 karat diamond flooded ring onto his pinky finger. "See... it's perfect."

Jay-Roc looked down at the icy ring and then up at Alana's sultry eyes. He knew exactly what she wanted.

Their lips clashed and their tongues intertwined. Jay-Roc reached over and palmed Alana's soft, round, brown ass and pulled her in closer. Their bodies grew warm in seconds and their heartbeats matched in rhythm.

Alana's kitty got moist when Jay-Roc squeezed one of her malleable c-cup breast and a sigh of pure ecstasy escaped her soft wet lips. She started unbuttoning his dress shirt and let her hands run over his well-built pecks.

Jay-Roc kissed on her neck and whispered in her ear. "I want you to ride it after I taste it."

Alana quivered. She loved the way his strong hands felt on her soft, smooth skin. "Ladies first." she said and slid down in the middle of his legs. She easily removed his belt and pulled his dress pants down to his ankles. One of her hands squeezed the bulge between his legs and she smiled. "Ohh... big boy." She tugged at his boxer briefs until they came down and then she buried her face in his lap.

Alana held his stiffened ten inches in both of her hands and sloppily sucked, slurped and licked while she looked him dead in his eyes.

Jay-Roc's breathing was intense. An intoxicating euphoria washed over his body and he gripped the back of Alana's head.

She went faster.

"Ohhhh.... shiiiiiittttt..." His eyes rolled and he almost slid right off the sofa.

Alana had his dick soaked in her saliva. She jerked and tickled the head making him squirm in his seat. "You like that?" She asked.

The only thing Jay-Roc could do was nod his head.

Alana got up, wiggled out of the tight sweat pants she was wearing and Jay-Roc pulled her back to the sofa. He put her on her back and got on his knees.

He stared at her freshly shaved vagina. "Damn you got a pretty pussy." Jay-Roc put his hands on her thighs and let his hot tongue brush against her sensitive clitoris. He worked two fingers into her soggy paradise and she moaned.

"Ummmm..." Alana's body trembled and she climaxed. "Oh my Goddddd!!!"

Jay-Roc licked her middle for twenty more minutes and she came five more times splashing his face with her sweet nectar. She had never had that may orgasms in her life.

Jay-Roc took the condom out of his pocket a slipped it on. "Come here."

Alana straddled him and leisurely slid down the length of his shaft. She forced her tongue in his mouth and rode his dick for the next half hour.

Jay-Roc picked her up and bent her over the arm of the sofa. He had to be careful because of her wound, but she assured him she was okay.

"Slap my ass baby... spank me!"

When he felt his explosion building he pulled out and she turned around and rolled the condom off.

"I want it all." Alana jerked him until he shook and filled her jaws with so much cum she almost choked, but somehow she managed to swallow every bit of it.

Jay-Roc stumbled over to the sofa, relaxed and a wide smile came across his grill.

"I hope you know how to cook." He laughed.

An hour later Jay-Roc, Malikah, Rahmeek and Loose were sitting in Malikah's living room discussing their plans for the trip. Jay-Roc had an attitude the minute he walked in and saw Loose sitting on the couch. For the first 15 minutes he kept his mouth shut, but when Loose tried to voice his opinion on something, Jay-Roc couldn't take it anymore.

"Yo, why the fuck did you bring this nigga, he ain't goin'."

"I go anywhere I wanna go nigga."

"Yo Loose chill."

"Stop tellin' me to chill Rahmeek, fuck this nigga!"

Malikah was fed up with the back and forth. "I'ma kick both of y'all outta my house if you don't shut up."

"You got something against my man Jay-Roc?"

"Fuck your man, Rahmeek." Jay-Roc grilled Loose.

"Okay... listen, we're meeting up with Deon's brother and sister early tomorrow morning in Mahdia, Guyana. Now, I've never been to this part of the country so don't expect me to be the travel guide. Hopefully we won't have too many problems finding them and everything should be okay. The flight over there is five and a half hours so if you've never been on a plane... prepare yourself."

CHAPTER FOURTEEN

-MAHDIA, GUYANA-

The three of them landed on Guyanese soil at the Mahdia airstrip just when the scorching sun was beginning to settle. The humidity was at a high 96% and scattered rain drops sporadically fell from the clouded grey sky.

"Goddamn! It's hot as a muthafucka out here Malikah. You ain't say nothin about this shit." Jay-Roc wiped the sweat from his head and came out of his shirt. "Akbar said he would be here. You see him?"

"How am I supposed to know what he looks like Jay- Roc, I never saw him before."

"I think that's him right there." Rahmeek pointed to a guy standing by a jeep. He was waving his arms in the air.

When they made it over to where the waving man was, neither one of them could believe their eyes.

"Hello, my name is Akbar." He held his hand out, but nobody budged.

After a few seconds Jay-Roc approached him. He studied his facial features and stared directly at him. "You look jus' like Deon." He was amazed.

Malikah hadn't moved a step. She dropped her bags and the more she continued to stare at him the more her feelings got rattled. Tears built up in her eyes as she thought about the day she and Deon exchanged vows. *Was this him?* The person standing in front of her resembled her husband in every way possible, but it couldn't be him because she was in the morgue when they pulled back the sheet to identify him.

"Why are y'all doing this to me!" She screamed and dashed off down the strip.

"Have I done something?" Akbar was confused.

"No Akbar. It's not your fault. She'll be alright." Rahmeek assured.

After a formal introduction and waiting for Malikah to gather herself, the four of them made the short journey into the village where Akbar lived with his mother and his sister Bibi.

Jay-Roc marveled at all the beautiful sights of the foreign country as they drove down one of the main roads in Mahdia.

"You see this?" Akbar pointed. "This area is called the Arcade. It has many shops up and down the street, food vendors, clothing vendors, whatever you want. My mother once ran a booth over here until she became very ill and had to sell it. This whole place is owned by a guy they call the Business man. He owns a lot of property here in Guyana.

"How did you find me?" Malikah finally spoke. She hadn't been paying attention to anything Akbar was saying.

"When Deon came here to bury his father he left an address with my mother."

"So he knew he had a brother and a sister?" She asked.

Akbar handled the jeep over the bumpy terrain. "Yes, he knew about us and we knew about him, but we never got the chance to meet."

"I wonder why he never said anything."

"I don't think Deon accepted the fact that our father was a cheater. He looked up to him. He thought he could do no wrong. When he was on the run from authorities he sent Deon and his mom to America and that's when he met my mother."

"And you said you got a sister too?" Rahmeek asked.

"Yes, my sister Bibi. She is at home taking care of our sick mother. She's so excited to meet you all."

Akbar pulled the jeep up to a wooden shack that was off a dirt road. To Jay-Roc the house looked abandoned and rundown, but to Akbar this was home.

"This is it. It's not much, but it's more than some have."

"Damn... this is some serious shit out here." Rahmeek surveyed his surroundings. There were miles of woods lining both sides of the red dirt roads and there were very few signs of civilization at all.

They exited the jeep and walked up three wooden planks that served as the front door steps. Akbar pushed the door open and called out to his sister."Bibi! They're here!"

The house was small, dark, hot and very uncomplicated. No pictures on the wall, no fancy carpets on the floor and no television; just a beat up am/fm outdated radio in the corner of the entrance space.

Jay-Roc didn't hear her enter the room, but when he looked up a living angel was staring back at him.

Bibi had a glazed bronze skin tone, extremely long, dark brown hair and beautiful observant blue eyes.

"Welcome to our home." She said, her voice, soft and innocent like she could do no wrong. "My name is Bibi." She stuck her hand out and approached Jay-Roc.

For a moment he was frozen in a stupefied trance, curious as to how a person could be so strikingly beautiful. It was like her touch brought him back to reality when they shook hands.

"Jayson..." He said, still in admiration.

Malikah and Akbar caught the vibe at exactly the same time.

"Yes, Bibi..." He grabbed her by the shoulders. "This is our sister Malikah and these are Deon's good friends Jayson and Rahmeek.

Rahmeek just stood around looking at the small cabin like living quarters. He couldn't imagine having to stay in conditions such as these. Growing up in the concrete jungle was far from the experience of growing up in the Amazon jungle.

"Yes, rest your feet. You must be tired." Bibi grabbed Jay-Roc's hand and escorted him to a seat in the entrance space.

"Bibi, go!" Akbar sensed a sudden change in his sister's demeanor and he wasn't happy one bit. He was very overprotective of his younger sibling and didn't want any man coming close to her.

"Yo, Akbar where the bitches at?"

Malikah sucked her teeth. "Rahmeek."

"I'm sayin' y'all got me all the way out here in the fuckin' woods n' shit... what am I supposed to be thinkin' about?"

"You sleep good tonight and tomorrow we go to the shops and then into the jungle." Akbar explained.

"The jungle? They got bitches in the jungle?" Rahmeek was dead serious.

Malikah tried to hide her disgust, but it was obvious.

After a mini tour of the 600 square foot space Akbar showed each of them where they would be sleeping and he also let them know that if they needed to use the bathroom they would have to go into the woods.

"In the woods?" Malikah didn't agree with that. "The women too?"

"Yes, I am sorry sister. If you need to go I will have Bibi follow you so that you don't get frightened."

"What if I need to go?" Jay-Roc questioned.

Akbar cut a sharp eye at him. "You are a strong man. You can go by yourself. Are you afraid?"

Jay-Roc sensed the tension in Akbar's voice. He didn't know why, but he was pretty sure it had something to do with Bibi.

"To be afraid is to be normal Akbar. Fear is a natural emotion that helps protect us and alert us to danger. So when you ask if I'm afraid... the answer is yes."

His first overnight stay in Guyana, Jay-Roc may have slept for an hour. He spent most of the night staring out the window at the stars and thinking about how exquisite Bibi was. He had never encountered such an alluring female before, but he also saw the villainous look Akbar gave him and the way he spoke to her, so the last thing he wanted to do was get him upset. He knew without him on their side, they were as good as dead out here in the jungle.

At 5:30am Jay-Roc heard footsteps approaching the entrance space where they slept, but it was so dark he could barely see who it was.

"Couldn't sleep?"

He recognized Akbar's voice. "Barely... maybe an hour or two. What the hell was that loud ass noise I was hearing all night? Sounded like a pack of dogs or something."

Akbar sipped the cup of hot tea he had in his hand and chuckled. "Those are howlers."

"Howlers?"

"Yes, howler monkeys, they sleep all day long and at night they group up and run through the jungle making those very loud sounds."

"You tellin' me those was monkeys making all that noise?"

"Yes, you will see when we journey into the jungle. Guyana's wild life is extremely broad. You will see a lot of animals you have never seen before and probably will never see again."

By 6:40am everyone except for Rahmeek was up and ready to take on the day. When Malikah tried for the third time to wake him up, Jay-Roc stopped her.

"Fuck it; let him sleep. He'll be a'ight." Jay-Roc stepped over him sleeping on the floor. "Akbar I'm hungry. Where can we eat?"

"We'll go to the market in a few, but first I want you and Malikah to meet my mother, then we can cleanse ourselves and head out."

Jay-Roc and Malikah followed Akbar to the back of the house which was only fifty steps from the front. He slowly pushed the door open and turned around.

"Her sickness is not contagious so you have nothing to worry about. Bibi, how is she doing?"

"Not good." She answered. "She doesn't want to eat anything."

Bibi was at her ailing mother's bedside trying to feed her hot soup out of a cup, but she wouldn't eat it.

Malikah couldn't stand to look at her for too much longer. Her skin was pale, dry and wrinkled with dark blotches that looked like scabs that had been picked at. "If you don't mind me asking, what's wrong with her?" she questioned.

Bibi stood up and placed a wet rag over her mother's forehead. "She has a severe case of malaria; one of the worst cases in a long time around here."

"I thought that only affected kids." Jay-Roc uttered.

"And older people too," Akbar added. "She's had it over one hundred times, but this time her body wasn't able to fight it off so easy."

"Damn... a hundred times? That's crazy. So, they don't have any medicine to cure it?"

"Jay-Roc," Akbar said. "Look around... this is not America. We are very poor here. I barely make enough money to feed myself." He picked up the cup of soup and sat by his mother's bed. "Bibi, take them to shower and I'll try and get mama to eat something."

Bibi accompanied Jay-Roc and Malikah out the back door and through a small bushed area, over to a spring that was hidden behind some tree branches.

The heat was at blazing temperatures well above 95 degrees and the sweat was pouring down Jay-Roc's back.

"Why the fuck is it so hot out here?" He wiped the pellets from his face.

"This region is one of the most humid parts of the world. We're right on the equator." Bibi replied. "It's even hotter in the dry season."

"Can I drink this?" Malikah let the cold water from the spring splash against her hands."

"Yes, it's safe to drink. Go ahead... shower."

"*Shower?*" Jay-Roc was confused. "This is the shower y'all was talkin' about?"

Bibi giggled. Her smile was infectious. "Yes, are you afraid?" She mimicked her brother's words.

Jay-Roc laughed.

"Here..." She lightly pushed him out the way. "I'll go first."

Bibi pulled her long hair up, wrapped it in a knot and stepped under the running waterfall. The light linen garments she wore almost became see-through as the water splashed against her petite frame. Jay-Roc couldn't remove his eyes from her lustful physique and she knew it, so she teased him and turned around exposing her perfectly heart shaped backside. If the two of them had been alone in these woods, the howler monkeys wouldn't have been the only animals making loud noises.

CHAPTER FIFTEEN

After they showered Bibi lead the trail back through the woods and into the house. When they got back Rahmeek had awaken and was up talking to Akbar.

"I see y'all doing shit wit' out me already huh?" He didn't even give them a chance to get all the way through the door.

"We tried to wake you up." Jay-Roc said.

"*Tried?*" Rahmeek turned to Malikah. "You couldn't wake me up?"

Jay-Roc answered for her. "I jus' told you we tried."

"I was talkin' to her."

"But I'm talkin' to you." Jay-Roc grilled him.

"Boys..." Malikah said. "Be nice."

The animosity between Jay-Roc and Rahmeek wouldn't be settled until they squared off. It was something that was bound to happen. The question was, when?

Akbar spoke up. "Malikah, did you bring our brother's ashes?"

"Yes, they're in my bag."

Jay-Roc passed her the bag and she pulled a black box out that carried an urn with Deon's remains in it. "Here." She gave the box to Akbar and a tear fell down her cheek.

"I can see this is very hard for you, but Bibi and I want you to know that this gesture means a great deal to us and it will not go unappreciated."

Malikah couldn't speak because her emotions were in a tangled web, but overall she felt better about the situation. She could be at peace knowing Deon is in the same place as his parents. "Thank you." she mumbled.

Akbar put the urn on the mantle and they gathered their things to make a trip to the market.

As they drove down the long winding red clay roads Jay-Roc appreciated all the sights, sounds and aromas of the lovely country. When he turned his head he noticed small groups of men trekking through the bush.

"Yo, Akbar where all these dudes goin'."

Akbar handled the wheel. "Those are the porknockers. They're going off to the mines."

"Gold mines?" Rahmeek asked.

"Yes, the gold mines. Guyana's economy thrives off the agriculture of sugar, rice, gold mining, timber and shrimp. Sugar is our largest import. We have the best resources in the world here; one of the richest countries, but we are some of the poorest people."

"So they go out to the mines and dig up the gold for themselves?" Jay-Roc was very inquisitive he loved to learn new things.

"Yes, but it's so hard to find a sufficient amount when you don't have the equipment to go in the ground. If you don't have your own machines you won't make any money. That's why most of these people get up every morning and come to work at the mines."

"How much money can you make?"

"Depends on how much gold you find. Right now I can get twenty five dollars for one ounce, but the big money is in the corporations. They're moving into our land and tearing it up for the gold and diamonds. They have all the machines."

"Sounds like what the pilgrims did to the Indians." Jay-Roc said.

"Very similar..."

Akbar slowed the jeep down and pulled over to the side of the street. Both sides of the road were filled with people at the market shops purchasing their daily goods.

Jay-Roc jumped out the jeep and peered over the scene. He saw so many bright, happy and colorful faces it made him want to smile. There were young, middle aged and old people milling about fulfilling their daily rituals. It seemed like everybody in Guyana was happy, but how could a country so impoverished and so broken give birth to a race of people that were so kind and polite? It was amazing.

The people were diligent and the pace was vigorous. The hustlers were running around hustling and the vendors were standing at their posts vending. Reggae music blared from every passing vehicle and police officers patrolled certain areas carrying high-powered automatic weapons. What surprised Jay-Roc the most was that the primary language was English, although it was spoken with a Caribbean dialect it was very easy to understand. In a sense it reminded him of being home.

They wondered the market and Akbar showed them all the different fruits and vegetables that the land cultivates. They made sure to try a few of the ones they never heard of before.

Before leaving, Jay-Roc stopped by a vendor who was selling fresh coconuts. He observed the dark skinned, dreaded shop owner hack away at coconut after coconut with a machete that was at least two feet long. He did it with a skill so crafted he could have had his eyes closed and he would still be precise in every swing. Jay-Roc had never tasted fresh coconut so he bought one and was amazed at how good it was.

Akbar picked up some vegetables, a few sweets and some fish to be served for dinner and the three of them headed back to the house.

By the time they arrived back at the house the sun was beginning to settle and light rains sprinkled down from the heavens.

"Bibi!" Akbar called. "We've returned!"

Bibi was in the process of brewing up a soup for dinner and you could smell the tasteful aroma from outside the house.

"Somethin' smellin' good in here." Rahmeek blurted.

"Bibi is preparing her famous pepper pot soup." Akbar explained. "It is one of my favorite meals."

After dinner Malikah was tired and the itis was beginning to kick in. She made her pallet on the floor of the entrance space and went to sleep while the four of them stayed up talking.

"Akbar, I brought you a gift." Jay-Roc went into his bag and pulled out the small box that Malikah gave him with a few of Deon's belongings. He opened it and grabbed the chain with the crown pendant. "This was Deon's, I'm sure he wouldn't mind if you had it as long as you take good care of it."

Akbar received the necklace from Jay-Roc and held it in his hands. "This is good gold." He said. "Was my brother some type of king?" He held up the diamond crown.

"Yeah, that's what we called him." Rahmeek answered.

Akbar eyed the piece of jewelry in his hand. He imagined his brother wearing the crown around his neck with grace and it brought joy to his soul. "I wish I could've met him and shared a laugh or a cry... something." Akbar was becoming emotional and there was no hiding it. "Bibi!" He called as he brushed the forming tears from his eyes. "This was your brothers." He passed the necklace.

Bibi looked at the pendant and smiled. "He was a king." She said.

When Jay-Roc looked in the box he noticed he hadn't opened the letter from Deon that was addressed to him, he'd forgotten all about it. He told himself when he got a few minutes alone he would read it.

Hours passed and the still of darkness surrounded the small house. Jay-Roc learned in his first 24 hours that the animals of the jungle come alive at night and make their own music. He tried to stay up, but the heaviness of his eyelids wouldn't allow him to and he ended up dozing off with the rest of the crew.

Bibi stayed up and sat by her mother's bedside musing over Jay-Roc. It was something about his presence that was alluring, mystified and far from the norm. He was different and she was very curious.

The shuffling sound of bushes in the back of the house caught her attention and she stood on alert. It was normal for a thief to sneak through the pitch black and try to steal whatever goods he could find.

Bibi looked down at her disease ridden mother and made sure she was asleep and then she went to check on the guest in the front. She snatched her machete that lay beside the table and went out to the back to find out what the noise was.

Blackness covered the jungle and the only glimmers of light were coming from the eyes of the night's creatures. Bibi stood at the back door with the deadly weapon clutched between her fingers and let her trained eyes skim through the dense, dark land.

She heard footsteps and gripped the machete tighter. The sound of leaves and twigs being stepped on got closer and closer and within seconds Bibi saw glowing eyes. She immediately made her move and swung the sharp blade with the force of a mid-evil warrior.

Blood splashed her face and the thud of a human body hitting the ground was the only sound to be heard.

CHAPTER SIXTEEN

Before morning came Bibi had to wake Akbar to come and remove the body from their yard. It was the third one this month and things only looked to be getting worse.

Akbar arose without making a sound because he didn't want to disturb the guests. If they were to wake up, how would we explain a corpse in the backyard?

"Akbar we cannot continue to live like this. I cannot keep this up." Bibi's face was strewn with splatters of tiny blood pellets.

"We have no choice Bibi. Where will we go?"

Bibi had that look on her face that Akbar had seen so many times.

"No!" He said. "How many times must I tell you, we are not going to America."

"But why Akbar? It is a much better life awaiting us across the water. Why must we continue to stay here and suffer?"

"Don't talk back to me Bibi."

"But why Akbar, why?" Tears of disappointment slid down her cheek.

Akbar raised his hand and slapped the side of his sister's face. "Go!" he yelled and she ran off into the house.

Akbar was done listening to his sister's cries to escape their country. He tried to tell her that that was the mistake so many people before them made and he didn't want to follow their blueprint, he wanted to etch his own.

He worked vigorously in the mine fields day in and day out to provide the necessary necessities his family needed only to have some thieves sneak in under the fall of night and steal it away.

After an encounter that nearly ended his life and his family's, Akbar set it in his mind that no one would ever steal from him again. So he trained Bibi to kill; he skilled her on how to use a blade so fluently it became second nature to her, a knife in Bibi's hands meant death was just inches away and it was sure to make its presence known.

Bibi wiped the blood from her face with a cloth, sat in the chair next to her mother's bed and the tears were still running from her eyes. She couldn't understand why Akbar didn't want to go to America. If they left now they still had a chance to become something and make good of their lives, but no, he would rather stay here and be poor, digging for scraps of gold and killing thieves in the night who come to steal the fortune he worked hard for.

As the numbers in her head multiplied she thought of all the men she killed and the grief cascaded down her face even harder. Her sobs gained volume and her heart grew wearied. She was fed up and regardless of what Akbar said, in time she would be on American soil.

From where he lay, Jay-Roc couldn't see, but he could hear delicate whimpers in the distance. He slowly got up to see what it was and the sight of

Bibi sitting in a chair crying her eyes out triggered an emotion in him that he never knew existed. He rushed to her side.

"What's wrong?"

She hadn't heard him enter the room and he startled her. "You can't be in here, you have to go." She got up and went to push him out the room, but Jay-Roc grabbed her arms and brought her close to his chest. She was inches away from his lips and he could smell the pepper pot on her breath. "Akbar will..."

Jay-Roc stuck his tongue in Bibi's mouth and cupped her ass cheeks in his hands. She kissed him back, but then pulled away because she knew Akbar would be returning soon. "Please go, Akbar will come and he will be upset."

As bad as Jay-Roc wanted to say fuck Akbar, he didn't and not because he was afraid of him, but more so because of his respect for Bibi.

He loosened his grip when thought he heard footsteps and when he turned back around Bibi was gone.

"You lost?" Akbar appeared from the shadows.

"I thought I heard something back here, came to check on you." Jay-Roc lied.

Akbar could smell a lie ten thousand miles away. "And if there was harm how would you protect us?" He looked down at Jay-Roc's empty hands.

Jay-Roc looked down at the 28 inch machete Akbar was holding. "What's that for?" He tried to shelter his discomfiture, but Akbar caught it. He took a step closer to Jay-Roc and raised the blade. The blood from the thief Bibi had just killed was still visible. Akbar studied the knife and then licked the blood from the tip. He tasted it and said,

"When you live in the jungle you either get killed by the animals or you become one."

————————

Malikah woke up not long after the sun poked its head above the mountain tops and walked through the bush to the small waterfall in the woods.

While she stood under the spring rinsing her body with the fresh icy water she heard the leaves crumble and then saw a figure moving through the trees. Malikah quickly snatched her shirt and threw it on, but by the time she went to reach for her pants she felt an arm on her neck. She couldn't see who it was, but they were choking her and the only option she had was to bite down on his arm as hard as hard as she could.

The attacker didn't budge. His python like grip got tighter and Malikah wasn't able to get air to her lungs, she started to choke, but with last of the last bit of strength she could muster she reached back, grabbed the attacker's balls and squeezed until his screeching wail could be heard throughout the entire jungle. The horrific cry pierced Malikah's ears and she stumbled back, bumped her head on a rock and passed out.

It was the next day when she came to. "Where am I?" Malikah lifted her back off the flimsy cot she was lying on and sat up. When the blur disappeared from her eyes she saw Bibi sitting in a chair about three feet away. "What happened?" She rubbed the back of her head, it was throbbing.

"Akbar found you passed out at the spring. You should never travel the bush by your lonesome, the jungle is a beast."

Malikah started to remember pieces of what took place.

"I went to take a shower..." Her voice faded and she swayed.

Bibi got up and rushed to her side. "Don't speak, I think you may have been attacked by a bushman." She gently pushed Malikah back onto the cot. "You need rest. You must sleep until your memory is restored. Here, this will help." Bibi picked up a cup with a spoon in it and fed Malikah some hot soup.

After a few more hours of sleep Malikah jumped from the cot in a haze, screaming like she was being chased in Jason movie.

Akbar, Bibi, Jay-Roc and Rahmeek ran into the room. "What happened?" They asked.

"Get my shit Jay-Roc, I'm leaving!" She tried to push her way through, but Rahmeek grabbed her arm. "Don't fucking touch me!" She yanked away.

"Malikah calm down." Jay-Roc went to touch her hand and she snatched a small knife off a desk that was behind her. "If you touch me I'ma cut your fucking throat Jay-Roc I swear to God."

Akbar didn't say a word, he just observed.

Rahmeek tried to grab her arm again and Malikah swung the knife and missed his face by inches. She had a crazed stare in her eyes and her breathing was heavy, she focused all her attention on Rahmeek and never saw Bibi make a move.

The machete was in the air on its way down headed straight for Malikah's neck.

"Bibi, no!" Akbar caught her in mid swing; it was the only voice she obeyed.

The two foot blade hit the ground and Bibi disappeared.

After they calmed Malikah down she rested on the cot and eventually drifted into sleepy land again. When she woke up this time she felt much better.

"I remember..." She mumbled.

Akbar sat beside her with a sharpening stone in his lap filing down one of the many knives he had lying around the house. "What is it you remember?" He asked.

"The waterfall, I was over there taking a shower when I heard something in the leaves."

"Did you see what it was?"

"No, when I turned around it was too late. He already had his arms around my neck."

"So how did you fight him off?"

"First I bit his arm—"

Akbar cut in. "You *bit* him?" He got out the chair and went close to Malikah. He pulled the skin under her eyes down so he could see the color of them.

"What the fuck are you doing? Get off me!" She pushed him.

Akbar stepped back. "If it was a bushman who attacked you and you bit into his flesh you can become very ill."

"Ill?"

"Yes, sick. The bushman have an unusually rare case of malaria. In the jungle we call it bushman disease and it can be deadly."

She paid full attention now. "What you mean deadly?"

"I have seen victims of bushman's disease die within three days of contracting it, but not all the victims die."

Malikah was on edge. "So what are the symptoms? Do I have it?"

"Your eyes are still of normal color. You may not have contracted it... or... maybe it wasn't a bushman who attacked you."

CHAPTER SEVENTEEN

"Jayson wake up, we must go." Akbar tapped on Jay-Roc's shoulder trying to wake him up. It was pitch black and when he finally opened his eyes the only thing he could see was Akbar's pearly white teeth.

"Go where?"

"Shhh..." He put his finger to his lips. "In the jungle. It's Malikah, she is going to be very sick. We must trek into the jungle and fetch some medicine for her."

"What the fuck are talkin' about Akbar?"

"When Malikah was attacked by the bushman she said that she bit into his flesh to try and get him off. The bushman have deadly diseases and I believe she has contracted it."

"Are you serious? Does she know about this?" Jay-Roc was up now.

"No, I didn't want her to panic, but we can save her if we go into the jungle and get her the medicine."

"What medicine is in the jungle?"

"Natural medicine. There is a tree called the Kina-Kina. It is a large tree with a red trunk and pink flowers. The bark of this tree can cure what Malikah has, but it is deep in the jungle and I cannot go by myself."

Rahmeek was awakened by their conversation and heard what Akbar said. "You wanna go in the jungle in the pitch black to go find a fuckin' tree Akbar? You must be outta your mind."

"This is to save your friend's life, are you afraid?"

Jay-Roc laughed.

"Fuck you laughing for?"

"Akbar asked you a question... are you?"

Rahmeek sucked his teeth. "Niggas from Brownsville Brooklyn ain't afraid of shit. Don't forget Akbar, I come from the jungle too, it's jus' concrete."

"It's settled then, Rahmeek you will follow me into the jungle tonight so we can get the medicine."

———————————

"I always wanted to go to America, what is it like?" Bibi sat in a chair next to the cot Malikah was sleeping on.

"It's nothing like this." Jay-Roc answered. "The people here are so friendly. In America, you mind your business and don't speak unless spoken to. If you follow those rules you have a good chance of surviving."

"But it must be nice to have so many opportunities and your own opinion."

"*Opinion?* What does that have to do with America? You have your own opinion here, don't you?"

Bibi dropped her head in shame. "My opinion means nothing here, only Akbar's."

"Why is he so hard on you?" He asked.

"Akbar is not hard. He is very disciplined and protective of his family. Shouldn't every man be?"

Jay-Roc was hypnotized by Bibi's eyes, he couldn't help but to stare and his gaze made her heart flutter and her insides moisten. He bent down to kiss her and she backed away.

"I see the way she looks at you."

"Who?"

"Malikah."

Jay-Roc turned his lip. "You buggin'."

"I watched her eyes. You can see what a person feels when you look in their eyes."

"Oh yeah, what are my feelings?" This time when he leaned in to kiss her, she reciprocated.

Jay-Roc lifted Bibi in the air and carried her to the front of the house.

"We can't do this." She wanted to stop him, but her body was yearning to be touched.

Jay-Roc laid her on her back on the wooden floor and planted light kisses all over her neck and chest area. He let his strong hands caress her supple breast and flicked her nipple with his pointer finger. Bibi exhaled a pleasureful moan of satisfaction, she had never felt like this a day in her life.

"You must be gentle." She whispered.

Jay-Roc let his finger slip into her running waterfall and she tugged at his skin like she was clinging for dear life. He felt how tight and warm her vagina was as he tickled her inside and sucked on her breast. His tongue took the southern route to kitty land and landed right on Clitoris Avenue.

Bibi couldn't hold it in. "Ummm... Ohhhhhh..." Her walls constricted and the convulsive shivers took control of her body. In minutes she had multiple orgasms. She didn't even know what the fuck Jay-Roc had done to her, but it felt so good she never wanted it to end.

"Watch your step, it's snakes out here." Akbar maneuvered his way through the dusky Amazon jungle with Rahmeek sticking close behind.

"Yo Akbar I can't see shit."

"Keep your hands in front of you at all times in case you come up on a tree."

"How far in we gotta go?" He was getting tired and more nervous as the seconds ticked away.

"Just a little bit more." Akbar said. "It should be around here somewhere."

"You said that a fuckin' hour ago Akbar. I ain't wit' this creepin' through the jungle shit... fuck I look like, Tarzan nigga?"

"Shhh... don't move."

Rahmeek stopped immediately. When he looked up he saw little dots of light moving around. He whispered. "It's something' out there?"

Before Akbar could answer, a deep, loud roaring sound filled his eardrums.

"What the fuck is that!?" Rahmeek stumbled and fell into a tree.

"Shhh... keep your voice down."

Rahmeek closed his eyes and silently prayed to God. He begged to make it out of the jungle to see another day.

"Those are monkeys."

"Monkeys?" Rahmeek didn't believe him. "You can tell me anything, but don't sit here and lie and tell me those are fuckin' monkeys Akbar, c'mon."

"Howler monkeys," He told him. "Ah ha, here we go. This is the tree we are looking for." Akbar ripped a piece of bark off the tree. "Okay, let's go."

"That's it?"

"Yes."

"You brought me all the way out here for a little piece of fuckin' tree bark, are you serious Akbar?"

The hike back to Akbar's house took forever because they stumbled upon a small problem. "Whatever you do, don't move." Akbar warned. "Labaria are venomous and they move fast."

"La... what!?"

"Run!!"

When Akbar and Rahmeek finally made it back to the house, everyone was knocked out. "Get some rest. Tomorrow we make another journey." Akbar patted Rahmeek on his head and walked to the back.

CHAPTER EIGHTEEN

The tropical rains came down heavy for two days straight producing roadways and hills full of thick red mud. It got so bad it forced the four strangers to stay in and get to know each other better. The in house experience allowed Jay-Roc to learn a lot about Akbar and Bibi through conversation and they also got a slight glimpse into his world across seas. Akbar and Jay-Roc shared a few of the same qualities and sometimes viewed things in the same light, but the one thing that remained a mystery to Jay-Roc was his future with Bibi.

Every night he stayed up late thinking of a way to ask her to come back to America, but if she said no, what would he do? How would he feel? The thought of rejection crossed his mind, but he pushed it far away from his brain and for the first time in his life he got on his knees, clasped his hands and bowed his head in prayer. He prayed that the love he and Bibi shared would be strong enough to carry them to whatever continent they chose. He prayed that whatever obstacles or setbacks they had to encounter would be worked out and laughed at as a distant memory. Jay-Roc prayed. He prayed so hard tears came falling down his cheeks and then the sign he just asked for appeared from the heavens.

"Would you like to be alone?"

At the sound of her voice Jay-Roc turned around. "Nah, jus' happy that rain stopped. I thought it would never end."

"And this is the dry season." She smiled.

"Yeah, I can imagine."

They were standing at the back of the house staring into the dampened woods. The rain had almost come to a complete stop and it was still a little bit of light out. It felt like the right time to ask her the question, but Bibi had other plans.

"Bibi, I—"

She put her hand up to his mouth and hushed him. "Follow me."

They fought their way through the small bush and into the dripping wet woods. When they came to the spring Bibi stopped and looked back to Jay-Roc.

"Do you hear it?"

Jay-Roc tried to listen. "What? I don't hear nothin'."

"The animals of the jungle are mating." She said.

"And you know that just by hearing the sounds?"

"When you live in the jungle for as long as I have, you start to learn the routine."

"Yeah, but--"

Bibi pulled him under the spring and kissed his lips hard. She ripped his shirt off and licked his nipples while the chilly waters doused their sizzling bodies. Jay-Roc removed his pants and Bibi let her linen dress dropped to the ground.

Their fingers interlocked and Jay-Roc pushed her back against the rock, Bibi raised her left leg so he could enter her.

She whispered in his ear. "Go slow. I'm pure."

Jay-Roc looked in her eyes and she guided him straight into the middle of her love. After some pressure he eased in inch by inch until their two bodies became one.

They made the most passionate love God ever created under a spring in the middle of the Amazon Rain Forest for three hours straight.

"Bibi," Jay-Roc was holding her in his arms. "Come back with me."

She broke his hold and faced him. "Jayson I can't, Akbar will not let me."

"I'll deal with Akbar, just tell me you'll come."

She watched his eyes. "Why?"

"Why? Because I love you and I wanna spend the rest of my life with you and you deserved to be loved. I see your eyes Bibi."

She shied away.

"You can't hide it, remember? I can see what you feel."

Bibi knew every word Jay-Roc spoke was the truth. There was no denying it, but Akbar would never let her leave.

"Jayson, let me show you something." She got up, grabbed his hand and they trucked deeper into the jungle.

"Hold on Bibi, it's gettin' dark. Shouldn't we be going back?"

"Do you trust me?"

Jay-Roc thought about it for a split second. "Of course I do."

When they stopped walking Bibi got down on her knees and started digging the dirt up.

"What are you doing?"

"Shhh... you have to be quiet."

Jay-Roc looked around. He didn't want any bushman surprising him out of nowhere, so he kept his neck on a swivel.

"Look." Bibi held up a small velvet bag."

"What is that?"

She got up from the dirt and poured the contents of the bag into her hand.

Jay-Roc's eyes lit up. "Is that gold?"

Bibi quickly shut him up. "If they find out this is here they will come and kill us all." She dumped the pure gold nuggets in his hand. "The gold is the reason these big corporations are migrating here. They come to our home and tear up the land for the gold and diamonds."

"It's diamonds here too?"

"Yes, those are the smaller white rocks. They have to be cut."

Jay-Roc picked up one of the stones and tried to see it in the dark the best way he could. To him the diamonds looked like rocks you find in a park and the gold nuggets looked like something you could eat.

"So, if there's gold jus' lying under the dirt why are there so many poor people in this country?"

"Majority of our people don't have the financial resources to bring in the equipment to mine these fields. We can only use what we have."

Jay-Roc tried to understand. "So, if you had the money for the equipment then you could dig up the gold?"

"Yes."

"I don't see what's so hard."

"This equipment is very expensive."

"How much is very expensive?

"One dredge to mine just this area can cost two million US dollars."

"*Two million?*" Jay-Roc did the math. If he could manage to get up two million dollars there's no telling how much money he could make. "And how much does the gold sell for?"

"At the moment one ounce of gold is worth eighteen hundred US dollars."

"What's your reason for showing me all this, what do you want me to do?"

Bibi had a plan. "Jayson, all this land is owned by my family and no one but you and I know this is here. If someone discovers this they will call in the big companies to come in and mine it. This is our land Jayson. Maybe you know someone back in your country that can help you get the money for the equipment and then you can hire the people to help you mine it."

"But why? What is all this about?"

"It's about keeping something that belongs to us, something that's ours. If you do this Jayson, I will come to America with you."

CHAPTER NINTEEN

"Malikah you got all your things?" Jay-Roc asked. They were packing their belongings and getting ready to catch their flight back to the U.S

Their trip to Guyana had come to an end and it was time to go home.

"Yeah I got everything. I bet you don't." She held up the lock box of Deon's that she gave to him.

"Oh shit, I was looking for that." He remembered the letter on the box that he still hadn't read. "Let me read this real quick. I keep puttin' it off."

Dear Jay-Roc, if you're reading this letter then I've gone on to a better place. Be happy for me, y'all the ones living in hell. Anyway, I felt the need to write this note because in the past few months things have gotten very strange. Let me start by saying this, every night I wake up in cold sweats from having nightmares. I keep dreaming that somebody's gonna kill me. The weird part about it is the only face I keep seeing is Rahmeek's. Jay-Roc, Rahmeek took the hit on me. I heard a conversation he had with some dude named Montega. After I did my homework, I found out Montega was Prince's man. If they kill me in the street, he had everything to do with it.

Jay-Roc's heart plummeted to the floor and he tried to stay as cool as possible. He couldn't have read it right, so he double checked and then triple checked, but every word was the same.

"What it say?" Malikah asked.

Jay-Roc gave her the letter and in thirty five seconds flat Malikah's face was soaked. She had been sleeping with the enemy.

"Where is he?" Jay-Roc asked.

"I don't know. I think he's out front waiting for us."

"Stay here I'll be right back." He went to find Bibi and Akbar.

Malikah cried until the tears drenched her shirt. When she heard footsteps, she dropped the letter and ran.

"Malikah!" Rahmeek called out.

He walked into the main room of the house and saw it was empty, but a letter was lying on the floor. He picked it up and started to read it.

Rahmeek grabbed his cell phone out his bag and powered it up. When it came on he dialed Montega's number.

"Don't worry Fredo... I'ma kill Jay-Roc just like I did Deon."

"He knew you wasn't playin' fair you fuckin' snake." Jay-Roc held the machete low and clutched it tight with two hands.

Rahmeek jumped when he heard his voice. "Too bad he didn't sub out earlier in the game. It's the streets Roc... shit happens." He held the letter in his hand standing there looking at all four of them.

"He trusted you didn't he?" Akbar questioned.

"What the fuck does trust have to do with it?" Rahmeek knew he was about to die.

Akbar ice grilled him. "It's always the one you trust the most that will shake your hand and then turn around and stab you in the back."

"Yeah, well he should'a had eyes in the back of his head."

Bibi spit in face.

He smiled, wiped it off and then licked it from his hands. "Did you tell 'em Malikah? Did you tell Jay-Roc, Bibi and Akbar how you fucked me the day of Deon's funeral, huh? Did you tell them how we been fuckin' since the day after he got killed? Tell 'em Malikah, go head."

Malikah stayed silent.

Rahmeek was slowly easing the pistol out of his pocket. He figured he might need one so the day the rain stopped he went by the market and found a vendor who was selling them.

"Y'all sitting here praising this muhfucka like he a king for real! I'm the muthafuckin' king!" Rahmeek was inching the pistol up more and more. "All the muthafuckin work I put in on those streets, he took all the credit and had me out there lookin' like a flunkie! Fuck that!"

Rahmeek got the pistol up hallway before Jay-Roc swung the machete.

His head bounced on the wood floor and rolled into the corner.

Bibi put her hands around Jay-Roc's while he still held the knife and slowly pried it from his fingers.

Akbar picked up Deon's chain off the mantle. "Jay-Roc... you got blood on the crown."

Jay-Roc received the necklace from Akbar and placed it around his neck.

"Long live the KING!"